I0687748

THE
RIVER

GRAEME SCHULTZ

THE RIVER

There is more to the river than you can see

Gobsmacked Publishing

Copyright © 2020 by Graeme Schultz.

All rights reserved. No part of this publication may be reproduced, distributed or transmitted in any form or by any means, including photocopying, recording, or other electronic or mechanical methods, without the prior written permission of the publisher, except in the case of brief quotations embodied in critical reviews and certain other non-commercial uses permitted by copyright law.
For permission requests, write to the publisher, addressed "Permissions Coordinator," at the address below.

All characters in this book are fictitious, and any resemblance to actual persons, living or dead, including events and organisations is purely coincidental.

Graeme Schultz/Gobsmacked Publishing

19 Trotters Lane
Cudgee, Victoria, Australia, 3265

Email: graeme@design2build.net.au

www.gobsmackedpublishing.com.au

Cataloguing-in-Publication Data:
Author: Schultz, Graeme
Email: graeme@design2build.net.au
Title: THE RIVER

THE RIVER
Graeme Schultz
ISBN 978-0-6484690-6-3 (paperback)
ISBN 978-0-6484690-7-0 (ebook)

Typeset by simplypublishing.com.au
Cover image by Susan Tara Meyer Photography
Editor Extraordinaire from the other side of the world Angie Zachary

For Angela,
wife and best friend.

To have your favourite person in the whole world
believe in you is the best gift ever.

Contents

CHAPTER 1

STEVIE

To say that Stevie Linden loved fishing doesn't go nearly far enough. Passionate? Obsessed? Does a bird love to fly? Does a fish love to swim? Now we're getting closer.

But even there we are missing something, because it wasn't just the act of hooking and reeling in a fish that he loved; it was everything about being there. The whole thing appealed to Stevie's more insular personality – not that he was introverted, but more that he was completely at home is his own company, just like his dad. Catching fish was great, but even if he didn't, he was still happy just to be at the river. That's the way he had been ever since he was little, captivated by nature's waterways and the fish in them – and that's why Stevie didn't need company so much; the river provided all the company he needed. All of which led to Stevie's frequent absent-minded musing about the fish and what they were doing – not just where they were so he could catch them, but what made them go from this place to that, and whether they enjoyed living in the river…and being fish, and so on.

Some people said Stevie's fascination with the river was a bit odd, but that didn't worry him one bit. He was completely happy inside his own skin; it all made perfect sense to him. And of all the waterways – the little creeks, the big river, the lakes and ponds, and the great ocean… he loved the river the most.

The river in question ran through the town of Allanswood, a medium-sized town that was pleasant enough in itself, but somewhat past its prime. Its prosperous beginning as the regional hub of the timber milling industry was long gone: the natural hardwood forests were mostly picked over and had been replaced by softwood plantations on the other side of the state. So Allanswood retained an impression of its illustrious past, but scratch the surface and the signs of a struggling community were right there. The township was loved alright by those who called it home, but the sparkle had tarnished a little and the dust of weariness had settled – like garden stakes in the vegie patch that had been left in place long after the crop is picked and only serve as a reminder of the successful crop of plump tomatoes they once supported, Allanswood was a town that had had its day.

The Hopkins River was no small thing, and it sliced Allanswood in half. The higher ground along the south bank provided for the important buildings: shops, churches, schools and the various public structures that lined the streets – with the best of them crammed together along Main Street, which looked out over the river. Main Street had buildings on one side, and the river with its grassy parklands and steep banks leading down to the river on the other – it was the part of town that most reflected the historic identity and prosperity of the old days. Bridge Street crossed Main Street at the centre of town and proceeded over the only bridge that traversed the Hopkins River for miles, so in the scheme of things the old steel bridge was recognised by the townsfolk as its link with the wider parts to the north.

The north side of the Hopkins River boasted no such illusions of prosperity, neither past nor present. It merely provided housing for the town's workers who tolerated living around the lower river flats and the occasional flooding that came with it, in exchange for house prices they could afford.

Stevie lived on the north side of the river not far from the sandy flats, had all his life. The river was just over his back fence, about three good stone throws more or less – just down a short track, and he was there. Which made it all so perfect because now that he was ten he was allowed to go fishing all by himself – he was allowed to go to the river and fish.

By now you will probably have picked up the importance of being clear on all of this, because it was Stevie's peculiar love for the river and fishing that got him into the unusual story that follows.

Saturdays were like getting out of jail for Stevie; he felt like he existed for just that one day of the week. Tantalising thoughts about Saturday filled his imagination all week long because he knew that would be his big day to really be himself – it was the day when all his hopes and dreams came true. He didn't hate Sunday through Friday; they just paled in comparison to Saturday so much that he dismissed them as unimportant – other than for their role in preparing for Saturday. You see every detail needed to be planned: where he would go along the river bank, what bait to take, and what weather to prepare for – so Stevie impatiently readied and re-readied his tackle while counting the days. All of the thinking and readying played an important part in the whole thing, not that he really needed to polish his rod one more time or recheck his list of items, but because the river seemed to speak to him when he did these things…it told him it was waiting.

For some unknown reason, the notion that the river spoke to Stevie in this way seemed quite reasonable to him; it was just a fact of life as far as he was concerned – as obvious as any other fact that didn't require further explanation or examination.

It was Monday and there was still a long way to go, so Stevie was not in the best frame of mind – *Agh, too many days,* thought Stevie, *still too many days to go.* He didn't know if he could wait five more days, but he had promised his mum and dad, and he had his school work and chores to attend to – he would have to try to be patient.

But the river pulled at him all the same, tormenting him with its closeness; he could almost smell the water, he could almost feel the breeze drop as he crested the river bank and disappeared down the other side, like stepping into his own private wonderland.

So Stevie invented games to get him through, games in his own mind, like little visits to his wonderland where he played out fishing scenarios in his head just so that he could feel like he was fishing before Saturday had actually arrived. He was good at this, inventing games as if they were real; he just zoned out and went fishing in his head until someone came along and shook him back into the real world.

And he had a lot of this ahead of him, because it was still only Monday.

No one really understood Stevie and what it was like to love the river and fishing so much. His crazy sister Kate who was loud and bossy certainly didn't, and even his mum and dad, who were more subdued by nature like Stevie, even occasionally made benign little jokes about how he was 'off with the pixies again' when he lapsed into his fish dreaming. But he couldn't help it; it just happened, especially on Mondays when it was way too soon to start working on his tackle.

Stevie had finished his homework and chores and was well into lapsing; he could smell the water, he could feel the breeze, he could touch the rod in his hands and the line sliding over his finger, all this with his eyes wide open, just sitting there on the lounge room couch staring at the wall on the other side of the room. He could sense the fish nibbling on his bait, its mouth wide open about to take the hook. *Come on, take it, take it,* thought Stevie, and as he felt it bite, he jumped to his feet and began to frantically reel in the fish…that wasn't actually there.

Unfortunately Kate saw him do it and laughed at Stevie so hard that she almost fell over; she roared so loud with laughter that soon Stevie's mum came in from the kitchen wondering what all the fuss was about, and she got caught up in it too and giggled out loud at Stevie's expense…which was most out of character for her considering she was normally so constrained by nature. I guess it was good to hear laughter in an otherwise subdued household, but to be laughed at for dreaming about fishing just didn't seem right.

No one laughed at Kate when she got all cow-eyed about some boy she liked, or at mum when she stayed up half the night sewing a quilt, or dad for that matter when he banged on and on about the footy – but they laughed at Stevie because he loved fishing so much.

It doesn't matter, Stevie said to himself, *I don't care if nobody gets me. They can laugh all they like; they just don't understand how completely happy I am when I think about fishing and how much I love the river and Saturdays.*

Some smirks were exchanged around the table that night at dinner; they were all in on the joke, and Stevie knew he was the punch line. Not that it was nasty or deliberately hurtful, but all the same, it's hard to be laughed at for the thing you love most…especially when you are ten.

He was just a regular kid, a bit skinny to look at perhaps, wiry like his dad but with his mum's big brown eyes and pointy nose – and this was the family he called his own, except they didn't seem to understand him very well. Maybe they had their own things to deal with, their own inner battles going on…so understanding Stevie didn't rate very highly in the scheme of things.

So he disappeared to his room a little earlier than usual; he yawned and stood up and walked out of the lounge room without a word and went and lay back on his bed to think about it all. He tried to reason it out in his head, *why didn't anyone get him?* – it was so obvious to him that the sheer joy of being at the river and fishing was everything anyone could want, but after a while he realised he wasn't getting anywhere, so his thoughts drifted back to Saturday and the river…again.

His mum coughed at the door and interrupted Stevie's thoughts; with a tentative and regretful look, she asked if everything was okay and said she was sorry for laughing. Stevie wanted to tell her about how real his daydreams were sometimes, and what it was like in that moment when he jumped out of his chair. He wanted to tell her that he thought it was old Eric the cod and that he thought he had finally caught him – but he didn't want to trouble her and intrude into her timid shell, so instead he just said, "That's okay mum" and wished her good night.

What was the point? Nobody got it – nobody else understood the river and all the treasures it held…nobody but Stevie.

CHAPTER 2

TUESDAY

Stevie woke with a start.

Someone is talking to me, thought Stevie … *or something.*

The voice seemed to be in his room, somewhere nearby, on his left or his right…he couldn't tell. He could hear a voice, but there was nothing there and no one, just his table and bed lamp, digital clock and glass of water. Stevie's room was uncluttered just like the rest of his life, perhaps even a little bland until you looked more closely at his neatly arranged tackle and lists – and an uncluttered room does not contain any hiding places for strange voices.

"I'm in here," the voice said. "Are you stupid?"

In where? thought Stevie, *there was nothing to be in!*

"In the water! I'm in your glass of water – I'm talking to you from the river." Then Stevie realised that the water in the glass was river water; it was pumped up to the house for their fresh water. The voice seemed to be speaking from the river and teleporting into his glass of drinking water…*amazing and also a little bit weird!*

"What was that all about yesterday? You almost had me. You caught me off guard, but that won't happen again; you're not a fisherman's bootlace, Stevie Linden!"

What!?

Stevie couldn't believe it; old Eric was taunting him. But what was there to taunt? Stevie was only pretend fishing in his head in a moment of daydream lapsing – it never actually happened…or did it?

"Give the kid a break, Eric, he's only ten," said a second, slightly huskier voice. "If you were as clever as you think, you would never have gotten hooked in the first place, only to be saved by a laughing girl."

"Who are you?" Stevie asked of this other raspy sounding voice, "I'm Leo; I've been in this river for longer than I can remember, and I've been watching you walk the banks, young lad, just waiting for the day you turned ten and could come here on your own. Well, Stevie, welcome to my world – see you on Saturday."

Stevie had had enough of this; he leapt out of bed, pulled on his dressing gown and slippers and ran down to the kitchen…*with the strange sound of sniggering fishes ringing in his ears.*

He quickly busied himself with breakfast, anything to avoid the crazy notion that he had just been talking in plain English to two fish. Even for Stevie, who was no newcomer to daydreaming, this was way out in left field – this was a whole other level.

So he did his best to figure it out, he tried really hard to think through what had just happened. He thought about the fish, and he thought about the river – familiar territory, because as you know Stevie thought about them a lot. He tried to place this new experience somewhere into his previous understanding of things, and his previous thoughts about what made fish go from this place to that, and whether they enjoyed living in the water, and being fish and so on.

But try as he may, this new experience fell way outside of his understanding of how things worked.

Stevie decided to take a different approach as he pondered what had happened: *Was it the fish talking to me, or the river? It might possibly have been the fish, because at least I know that they have brains and mouths, very small brains, and so maybe they had spoken because they had seen me walking the river banks, out there trying to catch them…or perhaps it was the river talking, which was less likely because it didn't have a brain – but also maybe possible, because it was so big and full of life, and other stuff.*

The speculations of a creative mind like Stevie's are endless and his musing about unusual things was quite normal, but this time he was stumped – this intrusion actually happened in real time and was not merely the product of his extravagant imagination. This time, Stevie couldn't retreat into the safety of his fantasy world because this was definitely no fantasy, and Stevie couldn't pretend otherwise.

The family were all busily preparing their own breakfasts by now, talking and eating and generally getting ready for their day all around him, so he snapped out of it and did the same. He put his thoughts to one side and got on with his day; it was like putting his thoughts up on the top shelf of his mind to return and take them down for further examination later, when it was more convenient.

But Stevie didn't return to these thoughts. He didn't take them off the top shelf for another examination; he just forgot they were there and drifted back into the normal flow of his life in the family and at school. Stevie subconsciously decided that it was all just another daydream, just another lapse of reality, and so he carried on as if it had never happened. He wasn't deliberately avoiding thinking about it; it was more like something that happened last year – it was real at the time but now it was just a fuzzy kind of memory.

The rest of the week proceeded without event. Stevie avoided river water…but not by any conscious decision. He didn't take a glass of water to bed…he just forgot to; and he didn't go near the river…he had other things occupying him. So the whole 'talking fish' thing drifted into a hidden compartment in the back of his mind.

By Thursday Stevie was full tilt into his preparations; he was absorbed with cleaning his tackle and arranging everything in readiness for the big day. Then after school on Friday, he could be found busily digging in the garden around the compost heap, collecting worms for bait – he would need at least a hundred of the little wrigglers for a full day's fishing. His last task before bed was to make enough sandwiches for a whole day away from home and put them in the fridge to be collected on his way out the door.

Everything was ready.

Now I don't want you discarding all of this as if it's a children's tale. It may well be a story about a ten-year-old boy, but that doesn't make it irrelevant to those of us who have a few more years under our belt. It would be a big mistake to think that way and miss out on the chance of looking into a world where impossible things might happen and do. So consider yourself invited into Stevie's world. Cut yourself some slack and be ten – you never know what impossibility might be lurking just around the corner.

CHAPTER 3

SATURDAY

Daybreak arrived right on cue, and Stevie was ready for it; he was never more fully alive than in that delicious moment in time at daybreak on Saturday when all his dreams would slowly begin to turn into reality.

Everything was packed and ready to go – rod, tackle, food and all the rest, and as soon as Stevie could see his way, he was off to the river. It was going to be a cracker day, just a hint of early mist coming up from the water, clear skies expected but not too hot – the perfect day for the most perfect activity of all – fishing.

Stevie hummed as he walked along, he even smiled to himself, he couldn't help it – *this was the best.* He crested the final rise and, at his first glimpse of the river, his heart missed a beat. It was beautiful – but more than that, it was oddly and mysteriously captivating…in a baffling sort of way. It seemed to be more than just a body of water quietly drifting towards the ocean; it was more like a best friend that he had been looking forward to seeing all week, and now as he stood on the last rise before ambling down the gradual slope to the river, he stared.

Stevie stood that way for maybe ten minutes; he was stuck on the spot, captivated by the strange wonder of it all, caught up as if in that first moment when friends meet after some time apart and don't quite know what to say. The awkwardness of the moment surprised even Stevie – much like a young boy who might be puzzled at the change in his childhood best friend when he notices she has become a pretty young adolescent. Stevie couldn't figure out what was going on.

Stevie had been like this before – captivated by the mystery and wonder of the river – but this time something was different, something had changed. He found it hard to put his finger on, but the earth seemed to have moved, tilted a little – it was the same river, curling its way through the same landscape, but it felt different… it felt brand new.

In fact, it felt so new that Stevie was rendered inert; he didn't quite know what to do next – which was quite something considering Stevie's eagerness to get started with his fishing only a few minutes earlier.

It puzzled him, because everything looked the same… but felt different. There was no change to what his eyes were seeing – it was deeper than that; it was going on further down in Stevie's consciousness – the river had, in some indefinable way…come alive.

Stay with me now; this is where the story takes on a life all of its own. Visualise the river that Stevie saw if you can. Get inside Stevie's head and picture this strange turn of events.

Eventually Stevie moved towards the river; he was drawn to it now more than ever. He was picking up the scent of a different bait…not the bait in his bucket, but the mysterious bait that was drawing him towards the river bank and reeling him in. Who knows exactly what was happening in that moment in time to Stevie – perhaps his vivid imagination helped, or perhaps it was more than that; but whatever it was, Stevie was spellbound by his once familiar river…that had now come to life.

And there he sat, on his favourite rock, and let it all soak over him. Stevie was a good sitter; he had to be –it came with the occupation. Only this time he was there so long he almost became part of the rock as the indefinable change to the river seeped into the deepest part of him, registering its strange new reality into the very heart of his being.

After a while his sister and her friend Bethany happened by, just out for a morning walk in the hope of catching the attention of some unsuspecting boy from school so that they could giggle and pout and do all the stuff young teenage girls do so instinctively around boys their age. Not Stevie; he was far too young to be of interest to them. But perhaps further along the banks they might find some off-guard lad more their age who was hanging about unsuspectingly by the river.

Kate walked over to Stevie and said "watchaupto", and Stevie shook himself out of his trance long enough to respond "notmuchjustsittinhere." "Catching any fish?" asked Kate, and then noticed that Stevie's rod was lying unused on the ground, and his bait was untouched. She looked at Stevie, and Stevie looked at her, and a silent message passed between them – he's spent the morning with the pixies again, and he's got nothing to show for it.

Stevie wanted to ask Kate if she had noticed anything, but he could tell she hadn't; she was just Kate being Kate, and the mysterious change to the river had passed her by. *The world has changed, and Kate and her friend didn't even seem to notice – how strange.*

The more Stevie sat and thought about it, the more he realised that it wasn't strange at all that Kate hadn't noticed anything. The change was happening inside him – the world was different because somehow he saw it differently; he just didn't really understand how that could happen, or why.

What is happening to me? Stevie thought.

The hardest part was being ten. He was old enough to go to the river by himself, but not yet old enough to understand what was going on. They hadn't covered this sort of thing in school yet, in fact he wasn't even sure that they ever would; nobody in his life had ever even hinted at this sort of thing. Stevie was on his own once again – not unfamiliar territory for a daydreamer – only this time he had no idea what was going on, or what to do next.

So, he sat on his rock.

He just sat there. He didn't try to figure things out; he knew that it was beyond his ten-year-old mind. So, he just sat and soaked in the newness of it all. After a little while, it occurred to Stevie that maybe he was just the right age after all when combined with his insular disposition. Perhaps this was happening just because he was ten; any older and it would all get bogged down in grownup reasoning. He decided to just be and see what happened next.

Stevie didn't know how long he had been there, only that the sun was high overhead and his backside was starting to hurt, so it must have been at least four hours. He didn't feel in any hurry to start fishing – it didn't seem important in the scheme of things – so he sat and waited and continued to soak it all in.

Sometime just before midday he heard the Voice.

It wasn't the fish talking, not Eric and Leo; they were nowhere to be seen. It was a quieter voice that he heard way down in his stomach rather than with his ears. Someone was talking, and he heard it with his belly. Stevie knew instinctively that this voice didn't talk to ears; ears were too connected to brains and too likely to misunderstand or misinterpret. So Stevie sat there and listened with his belly. He just let the voice say what it had to say and didn't interrupt by engaging his thoughts; he just continued to let it all soak in.

"It isn't what you think it is," was the first thing he heard.

Stevie waited for more; he knew there would be more if he waited, and there was.

"The river isn't what you think it is; there is more to the river than you can see…it isn't what you think."

That was all he got; the quiet voice had said enough for now. If it had said more, Stevie would have missed the most important bit; and he needed to get that, really get it, before the Voice could speak again.

At this point I'm also inclined not to say too much either.

But I will say this one thing: we human beings have a tendency to decide what a thing is before we have actually had a proper look at it. Be it a river, or anything else for that matter, in our own way each of us forms the truth out of our inner selves – very few have the courage to listen and hear and change the internal truth that we have taken so long to form. Children are better at change because they are not yet so attached to their thoughts; they haven't had the time to construct a version of the truth for themselves and take refuge in it, and so it seems perfectly reasonable for them to expect and embrace unexplained and impossible things when they come along…just like Stevie did.

CHAPTER 4
IMPOSSIBLE THINGS

Another hour passed, and Stevie decided to fish. His heart wasn't really in it, but you can only sit around for so long when the river is right there in front of you.

As he started to move about and get set up, he was distracted again by the river; so he absentmindedly wandered along the flats that made up this bend in the river bank. He just walked along, not really thinking about anything, passing the sagging bed of reeds that grew amongst the broken tree limbs, across the soft expanses of sand flats and over to the rocky outcropping that marked the point where the river turned back on itself and flowed on through the town of Allanswood.

His river was a big one; some people called it the Hopkins River, named after some big shot who owned land just below the bridge; but to Stevie, it didn't make sense to name a river after a man. After all, the man only lived near it; he didn't make it, or pour the water in – *Nah, this wasn't Hopkin's river; it was much more, and much bigger than that.*

But if it wasn't Hopkin's river, whose was it?

Whose idea was this river? How did it get here? And perhaps most important of all – considering the strange way it seemed to have changed – what was the point of it?

It might seem to the reader that Stevie was consciously trying to solve this mystery by carefully considering the facts and arriving at a well-reasoned conclusion, but that's not what was going on here – he was simply reacting to the obvious that was happening around him. The world had changed in such a way that all previously accepted information now seemed inadequate, and new information was pushing its way to the top to be absorbed and inhabited – again, like discovering that your best friend had turned into a pretty young woman…a completely different response to the situation was called for.

Without deliberately choosing to do so, Stevie had stepped into this new world. It happened without any conscious thought because Stevie was so accustomed to absentmindedly going about things that he just drifted in because it was there. Stevie had inadvertently discovered that the invisible realm was right there, just like the visible one, and it wasn't so hard to get in…if you had the inclination.

The new world was the same as the old one in every visually perceived way, except that it was inhabited by a completely different kind of life. It was a 'life' which was all at once tangible in so far as it was so evidently lacking in the old world, yet intangible because it was more like an atmosphere than a physical thing – a kind of dynamic all of its own – which was hard to describe yet profoundly there. By comparison the old world seemed to be declining and dying, whereas this new world was vital and brimming with vigour – and had a different kind of vitality that gave off a strange and foreign vibrancy that touched and reached into everything.

It was at the same time both disturbing and exhilarating, and Stevie walked along his river seeing the whole thing in a way that was so fresh and new it was as if he had never been to the river before. He wasn't trying to see it as new; it just was. He wasn't trying to fabricate this brand-new river out of his imaginary lapsing. This was no mind-game; as far as Stevie was concerned, the world had changed.

"It isn't what you think it is," Stevie whispered to himself.

"The river isn't what you think it is, there is more to the river than you can see…it isn't what you think" he mumbled.

Something caught his eye in the water about twenty meters away, and then in a flash it was gone. Stevie stared at that spot with all his concentration; he focussed in to catch the next sign of movement, but there was nothing, so he strolled on. Then he spotted it again, now much closer and ahead of him. He instinctively knew it was there; he just couldn't get a fix on it.

"Is that you, Eric?" called Stevie, "Are you messing with me?"

Nothing.

"Stop trying so hard to see me" said the voice in his belly. "We don't do that here. You're going to have to learn to look at things differently, to see the way they really are in our world; and the eyes in your head are not much use for that."

How else can I see things? thought Stevie.

"You have another way of seeing things built into you." the voice replied. "It's much deeper inside you, and it sees Life, not just things. Try closing your eyes and looking with your heart."

All of this Stevie heard deep down inside himself; his ears played no part in the process. It was more fundamental than that, more hidden away deep down beneath the layers. *Maybe I should stop trying so hard to see with my eyes, and let my heart show me what's going on, just like the Voice suggested,* thought Stevie. It sounded kind of weird when Stevie thought this way; it sounded like he was losing his mind, but it was that kind of day, so he went with it.

So Stevie dialled down all the stuff that was coming at him through his eyes and his ears, and another world started to gradually appear. It was indistinct, more of an impression than a clear view of things, but somewhere deep inside himself, Stevie began to see it.

Funny thing is, thought Stevie, *it's been there all along; I just couldn't see it for looking. It's the same river that it always was, but now I'm beginning to see into it. I'm beginning to glimpse the river within the river.* The reason Stevie couldn't see it with his natural eyes is that it wasn't a natural river; it had no physical form. Yet this river within the river was far more substantial than anything physical because it seemed to actually hold the physical river in place and give it its existence.

As I mentioned earlier, this information had a way of pushing itself into Stevie's consciousness without the application of much deliberate reasoning; he just knew it was true deep down inside himself. Some things are like that – they just are – and in much the same way that one might become aware of the existence of love because of its resonance in the deepest part of our being, so also Stevie recognised the reality of the River of Life because of a primal truth deep within him that bore witness to it. It seemed to have been somehow etched on his memory already, like an ancient cave drawing that was just now discovered, but had been there all along.

Stevie didn't know why he'd never seen this before; he'd been to the river often enough. Maybe it was that he was ten now; or maybe it was that he loved the river so much that had opened it all up to him. Who knows? The fact remains that Stevie and his relationship with the river had changed forever.

And Stevie also knew instinctively that this was bigger than the immediate environment in and around the Hopkins River, and that although it had all become apparent to him at the river, it wasn't limited to it.

There were two worlds, one seen and one not seen – and the unseen world was everywhere.

CHAPTER 5

WHAT IS GOING ON?

Sunday was a family day for the Lindens (that much was set in stone) – church in the morning at Allanswood Christian Life Church, roast for lunch, and generally hanging around the house unless there was some event or gathering to attend. On this Sunday, there were no big plans, so Stevie found himself in the back yard just doing what kids do when family protocols dictate the agenda – he was lying back in the hammock daydreaming.

Day dreaming has its good side and its bad side. Its good being able to escape all of the activities that vie for our attention by disappearing into our own little wonderland world by the river, but it's not so good when that little world begins to change, and instead of it being a refuge from the real world, it becomes a place with its own peculiar challenges.

It seemed that Stevie had landed in a place not of his choosing. Not that he didn't like the unique and impossible nature of this new world, but rather that he didn't know what to do with it, or how to engage with it.

What am I going to do now with all this impossible stuff? thought Stevie.

It's all very well to have a voice in your belly and talking fishes, but what is the point of it all?

An idea dropped into Stevie's head: *What if I just tried it out? What if I decided to live in the new and unfamiliar world for a while and see how things turned out…and would anyone actually notice? After all, both worlds appear to be the same from the outside, and I would still be me – it's just that I would live in two worlds now instead of one, and I could move about between them as the need arose. It would be like a daydream that was real…perfect.*

I know it sounds complicated when you put in down on paper like that, but inside Stevie's head it wasn't compli-cated at all. He was very used to living in an imaginary world where impossible things happened all the time – he visited there most days – except now he was going to make this new 'impossible' world his alternative reality and simply regard his old world as just his part-time place of residence. Stevie simply decided to flip the switch, to walk out of one and into the other at will; it just didn't seem all that complicated for a young boy who imagined alternative realities on a daily, almost hourly, basis.

He decided to give it a try.

Where to begin?

"It isn't what you think it is," whispered Stevie.

"The river isn't what you think it is; there is more to the river than you can see…it isn't what you think."

That's the starting point, thought Stevie: *There is more to the river than you can see…it isn't what you think.*

Stevie already loved the river; we all know it was his favourite place. He loved being there, he loved walking up and down the river banks just taking it all in, and most of all (you guessed it) he loved to fish. The idea that there could be more to the river than all that was hard to imagine, yet Stevie knew there was. He had glimpsed it yesterday when his breath was taken away by that first view; he knew it when he first heard the voice speak to his belly, not to mention Eric and Leo – so Stevie settled it in his mind once and for all: *there is more to the river than you can see.*

He had to settle it in his mind first; it had to be more than just an imaginary land – he had to decide that this new world was at least as real as the world he had always known…because this was not just another daydream… and Stevie knew it. If he wanted the Voice to keep speaking, he knew he would have to become a resident – and actually cross over.

You see, the River of Life can be seen only with the inner sight of those who have decided to leap across the chasm of their doubts; it remains invisible to all who hesitate or mistrust its existence – to them it is nothing more than a clever work of fiction, an exercise of someone's creative imagination which is nice to read about but has no actual reality attached to it.

In other words, there was no half way; it was all in or all out. *I can't be half wet,* thought Stevie. He knew that the Voice and the River of Life were more than just a fantasy; they were the most real fact of his life now, to be both fully embraced and lived in, or else simply treated as mere pretend play…there was no middle ground.

So Stevie decided to let go of his daydreaming and to give up his lapsing – he decided that this would not be just another extension of his creative mind; this would be the real truth in which he lived from this moment forward.

With that behind him, the adventure began.

Stevie had progressed from 'giving it a try' to realising that this new world in which the Voice and the River of Life existed was not merely an experiment into fantasy, not another pretend place to escape to when time or circumstances permitted – it was a place to relocate his actual day-to-day existence into.

And that's what Stevie did.

This is momentous, so I don't want to continue the story without first giving some deeper explanation. You heard right: Stevie has walked out of the world that was all he had ever known up until that point in time. Sure, he had regular excursions into his imaginary world before, but this was different. Stevie had now decided that he could actually live in this strange and new place (this other realm, if you like) while also remaining physically present where he was.

Sound complicated? As I have said before, it's easier when you are ten, and it might seem like Stevie is just lapsing a little bit further into his daydreaming world – but this was not like that. Stevie has actually determined that this fantastic new world was the real one, not merely to be visited from time to time…but lived in forever.

Now I don't want the reader to discard this information as we Christians are so often prone to do – as if the Kingdom of God is more of a positional reality or a thing we embrace theologically until the reality becomes ours at the end of our lives.

Like Stevie, we can't hear the Voice or know the River of Life unless we chose to make ourselves at home in the place where they actually are. Religion has developed a language around the appearance of living in the kingdom of God while actually remaining citizens of the old realm – but this is a leap way beyond that; this is a complete relocation.

If this book is about anything, it is about deciding to live in another place. Not just a place where the great big culture we call Christianity is, but a place beyond our wildest imagination – where God is.

Hold that thought! You will need it as we go along…

You see, in the same way that Stevie needed to 'get' that the river is not what it seems, we need to 'get' that the Kingdom of God is not what it seems. Else we simply engage in a more sophisticated version of religion, but don't actually hear the Voice or know the Life.

Okay, enough from me – back to the story.

CHAPTER 6

THE RIVER

As I was saying, with that decision behind him, the adventure began.

Stevie waited and listened. This was unchartered territory, and there was no instruction manual on how to go about this, no well-worn path to follow. So he got up from the hammock and wandered over to the back fence, climbed onto the middle rung, crossed his arms over the top of the fence and stared into the distance towards the river. He couldn't quite see the river from there…but he knew where it was.

This part was all new to Stevie. He was very accomplished at lapsing into a daydream, but had no experience at actually living in another world; so he waited for the river to make the next move.

It is just a matter of time, thought Stevie, *all I have to do is wait.*

In Stevie's mind, this was no longer a question of 'if', it was simply a matter of 'when'. He had crossed a line; as far as he was concerned, his decision to live as a permanent resident of the new yet invisible world had been made, the voice in his belly was real, and it was all the proof he needed. So as strange as it seems, Stevie simply expected that the new world would lead him on…into whatever was next.

As he stood up there on the middle rung, he noticed a strange change in his environment beginning to take place. He noticed the river beginning to drift in and cover the ground beneath him. It wasn't a river of literal water; it was more subtle than that, more like the invisible river inside the river – this was the life-source that made the more visible watery river so alive.

It was difficult to get a fix on this strange swirling river; it was unfamiliar and elusive, but one thing stood out in particular: it was good. It seemed to radiate a goodness that was fresh and foreign to Stevie, and out of that goodness emanated all that was necessary to sustain everything that was held within it. *How strange,* thought Stevie, *the goodness in the river has the ability to hold everything in place* – and he puzzled how goodness could do that. It seeks out and gives life to everything, and so everything seemed to be connected to it in some way, invisibly held in place by it – *the invisible goodness in the river is Life, and it's holding everything together.*

This river was rising; it was beginning to lap at Stevie's shoes, and its misty inclusiveness was coming up and up, gradually covering the landscape in every direction the eye could see. Stevie was beginning to feel like he was marooned on an island in the middle of the whole thing; he was standing on a fence in the middle of a swirling, fermenting river of inexplicable misty goodness. His house, the surrounding trees and other structures were way off in the distance now, just visible through the billowing mist – the river was beginning to cover everything.

Just then a head popped through the surface. It was Eric – he was teleporting again just like he had from Stevie's glass of water, speaking to Stevie from this strange river that wasn't actually made of water.

"What are you doing up on that fence?" asked Eric. "Are you scared of water?"

And then another head appeared alongside Eric. "Leave him alone, Eric, he's new at this – give him time, he'll figure it out" said Leo.

Two fish were talking to Stevie again…right next to his feet. They were real flesh-and-bone fish – cod, in fact – in a river of swirling mistiness. And they were speaking to Stevie as if it was the most normal thing to do, as if fish and people spoke the same language all the time, and they were just doing what came naturally.

"I'm not scared of water," denied Stevie, "but that isn't water."

"Of course it's water" insisted Eric. "Fish can't live out of water; what else could it be?"

Leo, who was much smarter than Eric and had been around a lot longer, explained it for both Stevie and Eric. "Eric lives in the Hopkins River. It's all he knows; he doesn't even realise that there is more to the river than he can see. And you're just like Eric, Stevie; you live outside the river, but just like Eric, you have always regarded the river as just water too. Both of you haven't realised that there is so much more to the river…so much more than either of you have ever seen or imagined."

Stevie looked at Eric, and Eric looked at Stevie "What is he talking about?" asked Eric. At some level, Stevie knew that Leo was right; he was beginning to understand that there is more to the river than he had ever thought. He knew that this was what he had been waiting for – so he mustered up all his courage and said to Leo, "Show me."

"You're hooked, aren't you, Stevie? You are beginning to believe. I can see it in your eyes – you have decided to relocate yourself into the River of Life, and now you want to see it. Good for you, Stevie Linden."

Leo went on to explain to Stevie what the river was all about. "This is not like just putting on underwater breathing apparatus and going for a swim beneath the surface. Eric already does that, and he still has no idea what he is actually in. But inside the Hopkins River flows another river, and that's the one you really want to see – that's the one where the real life is."

"When can we go?" Stevie wanted to know.

"You're already there; you're in it now" responded Leo.

So Leo patiently explained to Stevie that the greatest obstacle for people who want to live in the River of Life is coming to terms with the fact that they are already in it. Most people think it is beyond them, out there some-where – but it's right here. It's just like a normal river that flows before your eyes, but you have to decide to get all the way in it. It's a world within another world, but you can't experience it by looking at it from the river bank; you have to decide to get in it and live there.

"Take Eric, for instance" Leo went on, "he doesn't need to find the river within the river; it has already found him – he is already in it. The invisible contains the visible; that's just the way things are. The trick is to learn how to see invisible things."

Stevie listened hard, as hard as a ten-year-old could, but he couldn't hide his confusion.

"But Eric does need to see things differently and get a new understanding of what he is in, because without that he is just another fish swimming around in the Hopkins River. Eric has lived out his whole life oblivious to the River of Life because he only perceives what he can see – so the River of Life flows all around him waiting for him to see it and live in the wonder of it. But instead, he just lives like a fish that is contained by the ever-flowing environment of the Hopkins River."

"It's not as complicated as it sounds." continued Leo. "Once you realise what you are in, it will all be so obvious – some things don't make sense until you change your mind about them. The river is not what it seems."

CHAPTER 7

IN IT

The mist beneath Stevie's feet swirled and flowed. It was a mysterious current that was constantly moving, though not in the way the old Hopkins River moves ever onward towards the sea. This river moved because it was alive with vitality, and it was personal – it seemed to seek out and coax, to almost woo and draw him in – and it didn't flow out to the sea…it flowed into him.

The vitality in this amazing living river seemed to rise up and subside according to Stevie's reaction to it; it appeared to be waiting for Stevie to make some sort of connection – to say yes in some way. The river seemed to want Stevie…in an irresistibly good and inviting way.

Leo told Stevie that he didn't need to go to the River of Life because he was already there, and the willingness which emanated from the river told Stevie that was true…the River of Life was right there waiting for him. Whenever Stevie looked deep into the swirling mist, it lapped higher around his feet, yet never so much that he lost control, because the river was all at once strong yet gentle, determined yet loving.

All of this was clear to Stevie; he knew it in his belly, and he knew it to be true because truth has a way of showing itself if we are willing to listen to the Voice deep inside us. And as he listened, the Voice showed Stevie what to do next.

"Climb down from the fence" directed the Voice, "Come and discover the Life. Come in and trust me. I will not hurry you or harm you because I am gentle and kind; trust me to be good to you. You can't experience the Life you want by staying on the fence."

Stevie looked at the swirling mist and its continual mysterious movement; he saw the unknown in there and realised that within its depths lay a world unlike anything he had ever seen or experienced, a world that worked differently to his familiar world up on dry land. And the more Stevie resisted the river's call, the more the misty river seemed to retreat from him.

Stevie didn't want that; he liked it when the mist lapped at his feet. It gave him an indescribable sense of peace, almost like love itself was calling to him.

And that's what finally did it for Stevie: the love. He stepped off the fence and into the love.

First he stepped onto the bottom rung, and the swirling mist came up to his waist and seemed to tease him to go further. Then he stepped off the fence altogether, and the river came up to his neck. Stevie couldn't see into the mistiness even though it was right in front of his eyes; it was just too dense and hazy in there. But he knew deep inside him that it was safe – so he closed his eyes and ducked under the surface, feeling both elated and a little bewildered at the same time.

To Stevie's surprise is wasn't wet under the surface, and he could breathe normally, so he tentatively opened his eyes in the hope that he might be able to see something in spite of the impenetrable view from above.

Stevie saw the strangest thing; all around him was the activity of the river – fish, plants, and small creatures of every kind that one might expect to live in the river were there. It was a very busy neighbourhood indeed. It was all around him, but he wasn't 'in' any of that – he was in something far more intimate than mere water…he was in Life.

The ability to describe this new world would have been a stretch for a learned grown up, but for a ten-year-old, it was nigh on impossible. It was like Stevie had stepped out of himself and into a state of flawlessness – the old Stevie was still there, but he felt so new that he barely resembled himself.

It was more absorbed than felt. His five senses were not reporting these wonders to him; it was coming to him from somewhere far deeper inside than his senses could touch. By being immersed in the goodness of this new river, Stevie had been made good in a way that exceeded even his Sunday best; he had been made brand shining new. He felt that in some inexplicable way he had been returned to his true authentic self – reborn, if you like – back to his earliest origins.

As I said, this new goodness was absorbed by Stevie just by being in it; the river had washed him from the inside out. Stevie's only part was to hop in.

Perhaps all of this might seem like a rather intense and complex experience for a little boy, but that is because it is hard to find the necessary words to describe the scale and wonder of it in language that can be grasped.

In Stevie's mind, it was not complex at all; he had been undeniably transformed. He just let the River of Life wash him clean. All he did was let it happen…without putting too much analysis in its way.

And perhaps that's the reason why it is such a rare occurrence; people are far too analytical about the other realm and far too emotionally ambivalent about it, instead of simply trusting it to work itself out in them. They are too preoccupied perhaps with the theology of it and too engaged in the process, instead of leaning into the gentle and kind miracle of it. Being the naïve dreamer that he was, Stevie was able to bypass all of that, and as a result was washed clean by the River of Life as easily as one might be washed at home in the bath, he just hopped in and allowed it to have him, and so the deep cleaning of Stevie's heart happened quite spontaneously because that's what the River of Life does. But first he had to choose which river he would allow to have him.

Back to Stevie, his belly was hearing the voice again: "Now that you understand that the river is not what you think, we can begin discovering what it really is."

It's more than fishing and wandering the banks and enjoying the beauty of it, so very much more. Not that these things are not all good in themselves, but they are all about the visible side of things. They all depend on you and what you are doing – but the River of Life is really about something much greater than you. It is Life, pure and simple, and what the Life wants to give you that makes it special.

There is a Life in there that you can't see, and everything in there lives off it – most of the creatures don't even realise it's there. Like Eric, they just live.

Just then Leo swam right in front of Stevie's face and gave him the biggest wink. "That's what I was talking about earlier," he clarified. "The river is more than just water. In fact, it is more than all the living creatures in it too. Just because you are alive doesn't mean you have Life…you'll see," said Leo, "you'll see."

Stevie had been alive for ten years, and that was certainly no allusion – ten years filled with fun and games, family and friends. And in addition to that, these last few months since he had been coming to the river by himself, he had felt more alive than ever; yet none of that compared to today and hopping off the fence into love itself, and being washed from the inside out.

"I get it, Leo, I really think I do – having Life is being cleaned by Love."

And Leo swam off with a very smug look on his gills.

"Not bad for a kid, Stevie, not bad at all. I think you might have just figured out the whole thing about the river within the river," said Leo sniggering over his shoulder.

Sniggering fish, thought Stevie.

CHAPTER 8

BEING ALIVE

"Where have you been?" yelled Stevie's mother, "I've been looking everywhere for you. You just seemed to disappear, and I couldn't find you anywhere. I thought you might have gone down to the river and fallen in; everyone has been looking for you…I've been so worried, we all have, Stevie."

Linda stared at Stevie with an anxiety that came up from deep inside where her own inner fears lurked; she was almost beside herself with what might have happened, so close to panic that she was barely in control.

Stevie's mum had always been a bit tightly wound up; she seemed to live closer to anxiety than most people, and Stevie was used to it, but this time she was bordering on outright trepidation.

"I didn't go to the river, Mum, honest I didn't. I've just been in the back yard, I'm sorry I made you worry."

"We looked everywhere in the backyard, Steven; we called out and you weren't there. Now tell me where you were, or you will be grounded from fishing for a month," she exclaimed in a voice wobbly with fear and anger.

A deep sense of dread passed over Stevie…he just couldn't be grounded from fishing for a month, and he just couldn't stay away from the river…not now. But how could he tell his mum? She wouldn't understand – and Stevie wouldn't lie.

"Mum, there's more to the river than we can see," Stevie blurted out. "There is life in it, and it makes you clean…" Stevie stopped mid-sentence when he saw the cynical look on his mother's face. "You wouldn't understand," he muttered dejectedly.

"That's it, Steven Linden, you've gone too far this time with your silly daydreaming – you are grounded from going near the river for a month until you learn to tell the truth instead of these ridiculous made-up stories, do you understand?" Stevie gulped and nodded as he choked back a sob, hung his head and trudged sadly to his room, shoulders slumped in defeat.

How could the best day ever go so wrong? thought Stevie, *Everything was going so well.*

It had been a long time since Stevie had cried, more than a year, but that didn't stop him now – he lay flat out on his bed and cried and cried. He was just so heartbroken that everything had turned out so badly when he had actually done nothing wrong. Eventually, after what felt like a lifetime, the sobbing subsided, and he fell asleep from sheer exhaustion.

In his dreams, Leo showed up to give Stevie a boost, but Stevie just told him it was all his fault and that he could get lost and take his silly friend Eric with him. Even as he dreamed, he felt terribly alone; he had never felt this way before. The sense of loss and abandonment was over-whelming, and although he was asleep…Stevie despaired.

The Voice waited. Stevie knew it was there, but it would only speak when Stevie was ready; it did not push in, especially at times like this, but waited to be invited. And eventually, as Stevie slept, he began to listen as one so often does when dreaming – he listened with his heart. "This always happens" said the Voice. "Something always happens soon after you have embraced the River of Life, something that attempts to unsettle and disconnect you; it happens to everyone because the natural realm won't give you up so easily."

Deep in his heart, Stevie understood something about the river within the river; he understood that the old world we see with our eyes would always challenge the River of Life for control. The seen world would always seek to have dominion over the unseen. It was as if Stevie's internal wiring was trying to default back to its original settings…trying to get him to see with his eyes again, instead of with his heart.

"If you want to overcome anything, you must put your trust in the Life in the river" the Voice continued. "Even though it seems like everything has gone wrong, you must look away from your despair and hide yourself in the Love that washes clean. If you don't, then the old river will have you back again."

"The love washes everything clean; it is why the River of Life exists. Even the most difficult of circumstances can be washed clean, but first you must trust the Life that flows from that love, because The Great Love will never oppose your trust."

This was the first time Stevie had heard the Voice speak of the 'Great Love' – yet in his heart he had known that there was someone from whom it all flowed, and hearing his name for the first time lifted his heart with new hope.

"In the same way that the Voice will not speak without being invited, the River of Life cannot flow into and through your deepest despair if you don't trust it. You can ask The Great Love to do something, you can even beg or moan; but The Great Love is unable to act until you trust. That is why you knew in your belly that you had to relocate your existence into this new world, because you cannot be half in and half out, you cannot be half wet. Trust is an all-in thing, and you knew that when you stepped off the fence. There was no life in standing on the fence; you had to leave the fence to step into the Love."

There are times when sleep is the best place to gain understanding, and for Stevie this was one of those times – and as he began to awaken, Stevie knew everything would be okay. He didn't know how it would happen or how long it would take – but he knew deep down that it would all work out, and that all that had happened so far, as he made his first steps into the River of Life, originated because he was loved by the one called The Great Love.

Stevie hopped off the bed and wandered out into the kitchen where his mum was preparing dinner, "Hi, Mum," said Stevie as she turned towards him. "What's for dinner?"

Stevie's mum looked at him suspiciously. "Steven, I am not going to change my mind just because you come in here being nice. I wasn't born yesterday; my decision is made and will not be changed no matter how you act."

"That's okay, Mum. I know you love me and are just doing what you think is best for me. I'm not trying to convince you to change your mind, really I'm not; I'm just being myself."

Stevie's mum scratched her head in bewilderment as Stevie walked outside to sit on the porch step, inviting Shelley the cat onto his lap as he went. Shelley purred as Stevie stroked her, and a wonderful peace descended upon the Linden household, a peace that was beyond understanding. It was as if the storm that was raging all around had given way to a higher tranquillity, and it just seeped into the place without anyone noticing its arrival.

Stevie's mum didn't change her mind, and Stevie didn't push it. They both just soaked up the moment and allowed it to calm them and hold them in spite of all that had happened. Stevie heard his mum start humming; it was an old tune that she sometimes hummed when she was content – 'Moon River' – and Stevie thought how apt it was that she was humming that particular song about a river that was wider than a mile…*a river that made dreams.*

But Stevie wasn't out of the woods yet; his mum may have been humming 'Moon River,' but he was still grounded. *The important thing is not being allowed to go to the river,* thought Stevie, *but being in the River of Life. Trouble can't hold me unless I let it, even the troubles that upset me the most. All I can do is either trust in the River of Life, or not – and the Life in the river can only do its work when I trust it.*

A shift had taken place that Stevie was well aware of – the Life in the River could fix things, but it wasn't primarily about that. It was about being carried through everything both good and bad by The Great Love. Being in The Great Love was the thing; the rest was just the icing on the cake.

CHAPTER 9

THE LIFE IN THE RIVER

Monday rolled around again…so much seemed to have happened since last Monday.

Stevie wasn't in a bad frame of mind like last Monday; he was just doing his best to rest in the knowledge that the River of Life would work everything out – he was trying to walk out this new life, but there was no one to turn to for advice.

It was tricky because he had to focus on his schoolwork and his chores around the house too. He had to be a part of the family and connect with the circle of love at home – but he also needed to stay in the river and keep trusting in the Life that was there. Stevie figured that the River of Life had started this whole thing, and all he could do would be to get out of the way and just let the river be the river and do what it does best. He would simply stand back and trust…and see what happened.

Linda Linden was just an ordinary woman who loved stitching; the repetition of it soothed her and went some way towards filling the emptiness she had known most of her life. The emptiness was always present, and it had shrunk Linda's personality to the point where she seemed almost colourless. Even her stature seemed to be hemmed in by it, to the point where she passed through life without leaving any lasting impression upon anyone… she was just there. Her way of adding back some colour was in her creative craft work; it seemed to be an expression of someone who lived deep inside her but was otherwise invisible to the outside world.

"Stevie, can you help me with this?" Linda asked her son; she was trying to move the kitchen table over near the window so she could do some needle work in the light. Together they dragged the table across the room and let out a big sigh when it was in place.

"What are you making, Mum?" asked Stevie.

"It's a wall hanging I've been planning for a while," she said, "a kind of patchwork mural about where we live and our surroundings."

"Will the river be in it?" asked Stevie with a sudden increased interest.

"I guess so," she responded. "Life wouldn't be the same without the river; it's a part of us."

Stevie smiled; the river seemed to weave its way into every conversation. *Yes, it really is a part of us,* he thought.

After completing his outside chores, feeding the chooks and emptying the bins, Stevie returned to the kitchen to see how his mum was getting on. "Stevie, I have pencilled in the house and the yard up to the back fence, but I can't picture the river very well. Can you sketch it for me?"

Stevie was more of a dreamer than a sketcher, but the subject matter was so familiar to him that he answered confidently, "Sure I can, Mum." He talked as he sketched.

"You have to follow the path out the back, then cross the rise and there is the river. The rock I sit on is directly in front of you, on the left is the wide part of the river that heads upstream, and on the right is the broken tree, then the sand flats, and finally the rocky outcrop where the river turns back on itself and heads into town – just like that." And with that Stevie had sketched the river, and filled up the top third of the mural.

"My, my" remarked Linda, a bit surprised. "You do know the river very well, don't you?"

And Stevie nodded and answer with a smile, "I love it."

"Tell me about the river," said Linda absent-mindedly, "tell me why you love it so." Linda was concentrating on her work and chatting with Stevie without and real intent; she was just conversing because he was there.

"Mum, are you sure you want me to tell you about the river? Last time I did, it got me in big trouble."

That pulled Linda's attention into the conversation. She scratched her head as she often did when thinking and answered, "Let's just talk about it and see where it takes us. This is to help me with the mural, not to explain why you went missing yesterday, okay?"

"I do love the river, Mum, and I know I daydream about it a lot, but I think about it even when I'm not daydreaming too, just like you think about your next stitching project. Sometimes I see you thinking as you stand at the sink and stare out the kitchen window."

"Well, really" said Linda, "I didn't think anyone noticed, especially you, my little daydreamer. I thought you were too busy thinking about fishing to notice anything else much," she commented as she ruffled Stevie's mop of hair. "Maybe I'm a daydreamer just like you Stevie; maybe we are both inclined to lapse into our own little worlds that bring us pleasure…and I guess there are the other things the press into our minds from time to time too."

Stevie took that as all the permission he needed and launched into explaining all about the river. He talked about the sights and the sounds, the conversations he had with those who passed by and those he had with himself when no one else was there – and he talked about catching fish, and the joy of waiting and watching. And especially he talked about the sheer thrill of pulling in a fish and landing it and holding it in his hands, he even mentioned Eric the cod and their ongoing battle of wits.

After he had rambled on like that for about ten minutes, he just sat there and let the wonder of it fill him. He just sat there with his mum and the moment overwhelmed him, and he smiled without really meaning to.

Linda noticed. "Is there more, Stevie? I feel like there is something you haven't said yet…am I right, Stevie – is there more you want to say?"

"Are you really sure, Mum?" asked Stevie uncertainly. "This is what got me in trouble, and I don't want to make things worse."

"Okay, let's make a deal" suggested Linda, "You can say whatever you want, and I won't let it make things worse – besides, I want to know what is going on inside that cute little head of yours."

So Stevie explained it like this. "I love fishing, and I love the river, but there is something more to it than that.

There is another river inside the river that you can't see with your eyes." Stevie glanced at his mum to make sure that cynical look hadn't reappeared. "It's like another world that talks to the very deepest inside part of me." He cast another glance just to check.

"Hmmm," murmured Linda, "that's interesting. Let me think about that while I'm stitching, and I might ask you some more questions later. Can you get me a glass of water, Stevie?"

Stevie looked up. "Are we okay with this, Mum? I haven't made you mad?"

"You haven't made me mad," said Linda wistfully, and Stevie noticed as he wandered over to the sink that she was staring out the window like she sometimes did.

Stevie had noticed she stared out of the window at times and appeared to be looking at something far off in the distance, yet he knew that she wasn't looking at the landscape, but at something hidden deep inside herself. He didn't realise that she was trying to resolve something from her past that reflected on her face like a deep sadness or loss from long ago.

A few hours later, Stevie came back inside for dinner. The table was still pushed up against the window, so it looked like they would be eating dinner on their laps in front of the television. Linda caught Stevie's eye as she was serving up the food and gave him a wink. "Go wash up for dinner, honey," she said with one of her big smiles normally reserved for very special occasions.

Wow, thought Stevie, *that was a big smile; I wonder what's going on.*

Not much more was said about the subject for days. Stevie and Linda smiled at each other a lot, but that was it – they didn't seem to be able to find any more words for the moment, so they just enjoyed being together and working on the wall hanging. The was no more talk of the river or Stevie's conversation about it, but they both knew something had passed between them as a result of that conversation, and the poignancy of the moment lingered.

By Thursday the atmosphere between them was alive with promise. The unspoken energy which passed between them spoke more than a thousand words could, and yet neither of them had done a thing to make it so. It was an atmosphere unfamiliar to them both and completely in contrast to their normally subdued relationship.

Eventually it became too much for Linda, and she finally broached the subject. "Stevie, you are still grounded. We both know that, but I would like to suggest a compromise – you can go to the river on Saturday…but no fishing." And then, as if it was just an afterthought, "…and I would like to come with you."

By now, Stevie was getting quite accustomed to not saying much, so he just nodded his head and smiled a smile so big that it even outdid his mum's.

CHAPTER 10

THE RIVER – PART 2

Saturday again, but with a difference – no fishing rod, no tackle and no bait. Just a packed lunch with a few extra fancy bits thrown in by Linda.

Stevie still didn't know what was going through his mum's mind; they hadn't returned to the subject on Monday or at any time since. They just had an unspoken pact that something was happening which neither of them wanted to unsettle by talking about it; they didn't want to give it form before it was ready – a bit like taking a cake out of the oven too soon. Both of them in their own way were quietly excited; it was an anticipation that a beautiful thing was taking place, and they were both more than ready to let it happen.

Stevie didn't normally hold his mum's hand – he was much too old for that now – but as they set off, he gently placed his hand in hers, and she gave it a little squeeze just to confirm that she was thinking the same thing. Off they went, down the path to the river, just two people walking hand in hand wondering what the day ahead might hold…two people between whom had passed a depth of understanding that neither had fashioned, and that in its own way had surprised them both by the tender unspoken way it had linked their hearts.

Stevie could barely contain himself. He wanted to run, he wanted to skip or jump, anything to give expression to the joy inside him; but he held it in as he smiled to himself and began the gentle climb up the last rise before the river. If Stevie had looked he would have seen the same smile on his mum's face too.

Just before they were able to see the river, Stevie said, "Close your eyes, Mum, and I will walk you up; don't open them until I say so." So she did, and Stevie led her the last ten meters hand in hand to the top of the rise.

Before Stevie could tell Linda to open her eyes, she spoke. "Stevie, I can't open my eyes yet. I think I need to listen for a little while…someone is trying to talk to me."

It was like Stevie's first experience all over again, yet it seemed even more intense in Linda – she was completely struck dumb. Linda couldn't speak if she had wanted to because the Voice was showing her the truth – about herself, about her life and the distant but ever-present pain in it…and about the River that was Life.

Linda stood like that for a long time. Stevie had let go of her hand and sat on the ground almost an hour ago; he just sat there and waited for his mum to move. Eventually she held out her hand and mumbled, "Stevie, take me home." As Stevie looked closer, he could see that Linda's eyes were still shut tight; she needed to be led home by the hand…he would have to guide the way back.

Stevie led Linda home. She hadn't opened her eyes to see the river. In fact, she had hardly spoken, and now they were going back the same way they had come, except Linda's eyes were shut. As they neared the house, Linda told her son, "Stevie, take me to my armchair in the lounge room and then leave me alone for the day. Your grounding has finished; you can go fishing."

Stevie opened the back gate and led his mum into the house and to her chair as she had asked, but as Stevie left the room, he heard his mother begin sobbing. He couldn't leave her like that; in spite of his urgent desire to go fishing, it seemed wrong to just walk out of the house and leave his mum in such sadness and distress, so he sat quietly on the back step and waited with the cat.

He wondered what had happened, and whether this thing that was causing his mum to cry was a good thing or a bad thing. He wondered most of all whether he had been wrong in taking her to the river. But it was Linda's idea to go, not his, and she seemed to know that it was important; so Stevie let it rest and lapsed into daydreaming.

The mist started forming around Stevie again, wisps of movement like the motion of a river, lapping at his shoes, then his legs and waist. Stevie was sitting down, so it engulfed him quickly. In just a few moments, he found himself in the flow again, being washed and being loved, all of his concerns for his mother rinsed clean by the river which is Love.

Stevie looked around him to see what was happening and noticed someone off in the distance, a little girl dancing in the love. She was jumping and leaping with all her heart, and embracing the joy of the moment with all she had inside her. Stevie was drawn to her and walked slowly over to where she danced. She was beautiful…so full of life, so radiant, so alive. She was young, maybe four years old, and she was so very happy. She looked familiar to Stevie, but he couldn't place her, so he asked her name.

"I'm Linda, silly, you know me!" And all at once, he did.

"But why are you here?" asked Stevie, confused, "and why are you such a little girl?"

Linda looked puzzled with Stevie's line of questioning. It seemed perfectly obvious – she was here to set grown-up Linda free. "The Voice is speaking to grown-up Linda now; he is taking her back to that day, the day when her heart was shattered into a million tiny pieces, the day when her mother was killed before her very eyes by a speeding car…the day when she was me."

A tear escaped little Linda's eye, and then she said, "Come; come with me, and we will set her free."

Deep inside Stevie had always known that his mother carried a burden – not that she had said anything or made a fuss, but the way she stared through the kitchen window was at times, though not always, heavy with sorrow…at those times, the feeling of her sadness filled the room. And now he knew why, and he knew that she had been imprisoned in that moment – trapped in a loss too sad for words and too impossible for her to resolve on her own.

"How can we set her free?" asked Stevie.

"Come and see what The Great Love will do."

They approached grown-up Linda still sitting in her lounge chair, her eyes still closed, and she was surrounded by the misty river without even realising it; it was swirling around her and lapping gently at her hands and face.

"Her heart is trapped in the old river; that's where the terrible event is kept," explained little Linda with an understanding beyond her years. "We are going to set her free into the new one. She is trapped in death, and we are going to take her away from that into the River of Life." With that little Linda climbed up into grown-up Linda's lap, and she gently kissed her and leaned deeply into her and cried. And as she did, grown-up Linda began to cry as well, and slowly the two of them cried away all their tears. When one cried, the other would cry as well, and when they had cried, and then cried some more, it was over, and all the tears were all shed.

Then The Great Love collected all the tears, every drop that had been cried by the little girl and the grown-up woman, and all those in the years in between, and The Great Love added to those tears even more tears of his own. But The Great Love's river of tears had life in them; they were mysterious and powerful tears that overflowed from a heart so full of love that all the sorrow was changed into a tender and joyful peace.

As Stevie watched, little Linda slid off grown-up Linda's lap and, as her feet touched the floor, she danced with all her might. Around and around grown-up Linda she danced, twirling and leaping for the sheer joy that comes only from knowing that you are loved with a great love. And when she had finished, she reached up on her toes and kissed Stevie on the cheek and skipped off into the mist.

Stevie was exhausted. It was all too much to take in, so he slumped down onto the floor, resting his head on his mum's leg, and fell asleep.

Stevie felt his mum stirring and came awake as well, and as they looked at each other, they both smiled their biggest smiles. *I think she knows that I know,* thought Stevie. Linda wasn't ready to talk about it, but there was a fresh and new glow about her that Stevie had never seen before; the sorrow of a lifetime was gone.

She looked so new, it was like she had just been born.

…now, I want you to hold that thought.

It's much too early to draw conclusions about anything just yet. Let the river continue to explain itself as the story goes along.

CHAPTER 11

LINDA

Sunday began like any other Sunday. The Linden family gathered in the kitchen for breakfast, and it was just a normal, peaceful morning of relaxed togetherness before getting ready for church. There was conversation, but not too much; each person was just doing their own thing or lost in their own thoughts in the unhurried atmosphere.

Linda Linden liked her name; she secretly liked the quirkiness of it and that it contrasted so much of her life. She quietly wanted to be more colourful and, for the first time in ages, she began to indulge her imagination in that; and she was whistling again – they hadn't heard that for a long time either.

Dad was reading the Sunday paper. He looked over at Stevie and grinned. It was so nice to be together in this happy place, and each of them could feel it. Something good had settled on the household, and each one of them let it take hold of them. They didn't need to analyse it; they just basked in the warmth of it.

"Stevie isn't grounded anymore, Art," Linda remarked to her husband.

"Oh, why is that?" asked Art.

"It just is," stated Linda calmly. "I just knew inside it was right to end it, so I did." Art didn't need to respond;

Linda had instigated the grounding and she could end it. It was fine with him. Besides, the air of peace and contentment in the house seemed to reinforce to Art that this decision was part of something bigger that was going on, and he liked it whatever it was.

He and Linda had been childhood sweethearts; they had grown up together in Allanswood and had become so comfortable together as young people that they never felt the need to explore other relationships. So they married young, finding the refuge they both needed in each other, and settled into a life that was stable – and perhaps a little unexciting. Most of the time, that suited them because a bigger life came with too many risks and challenges; so they hid themselves away in ordinariness, and only from time to time wondered what life was like outside those safe confines.

"Do we have any plans for this afternoon?" asked Art. "It seems like such a beautiful day that we should all do something together."

"Hmmm" said Linda, "Leave it with me. Something will come to mind before lunch time. Let's go to church and see if any ideas pop up between now and then." So they did. The Linden family went to church as always and left the afternoon plans in Linda's hands.

"What about a picnic at the river," enquired Linda in the car on the way home from church. "We can have it ready in about half an hour if we all pitch in, and then we can all walk down." The day was shaping up to be sunny, in the mid-twenties, no wind, and just enough cloud to break up the glare of the sun…perfect.

This time, as they set off, Stevie restrained himself from holding his mum's hand…it wasn't that he didn't want to, but his dad was already holding her hand – something else he hadn't seen in quite a long time.

As they crested the last rise, Linda exclaimed, "It's so beautiful! I haven't seen the river for so long."

Art looked at her, a little puzzled, "I thought you were here with Stevie yesterday" he said.

"Yes, I was, Art," replied Linda thoughtfully, "but I didn't see the river. I didn't open my eyes the whole time."

"I don't understand," replied Art. "You didn't open your eyes and look at the river at all? Not even as you were walking up to it like we are now? That's a bit odd, Linda."

Linda took a deep breath and began to explain. She covered everything from the strange feeling she had when she and Stevie had first talked about the life in the river, all the way to when she cried her way through the loss of her mother and the gentle way The Great Love took her pain away. "I couldn't open my eyes the whole time until it was over because it was happening so deeply inside my heart," she explained.

Art listened intently but with a slightly perplexed frown on his face. "Well, I don't really understand much of that, but I can see you are much more content than you have been in a long time – so let's all just enjoy the river and our picnic on this most glorious day."

Linda knew that Art didn't really believe all she had said, at least not deep down, but that was okay; she hadn't believed Stevie either when he first tried to explain it. Best to just let it rest and enjoy each other… best to just let the river decide what's best for everyone.

So they picnicked and wandered the river banks, and then lay around and dozed in the sun on the picnic rug. Linda and Art stretched out while the kids were off throwing pebbles and generally loitering about. Linda had her head in the crook of Art's arm with her sun hat drooped over her face, and as the sun warmed her all over, she drifted off to sleep. Art was comfortable too; cradling Linda's head was so relaxing, and the closeness of her filled him with a deep contentment. So he drifted off as well.

They both slept lightly, aware of their surroundings but lulled into the drowsiness of the sun high above as it gently warmed them. Linda half dreamed, the sort of dream that you are not quite in – and not quite not in. It was a dream about being a child again and how her sadness had overshadowed the joy all around her, how it had shaped her impressions of the world and remoulded her world into the shape of her sadness. She found herself reliving moments from her childhood, experiencing them again as an observer might experience an event in the distance, and watching herself interpreting those events as if her pain was a filter through which they must all pass.

Linda didn't attempt to change the scenes that were unfolding before her; she just watched it all happening and, in the watching, she began to understand herself better. She began to understand that her pain had formed around her its own peculiar reality, and that there was actually so much more taking place than her pain had allowed through. Her pain had chosen how her mind would perceive life, and she realised now that, in spite of herself, she had no say in the matter.

It comforted Linda to know this because it explained a lot, and it gave her hope for the future.

As she was drifting through this slumbering epiphany, a loud noise erupted, like a bear or a pig in fright about to attack her. She woke with a start and looked around, then realised it was just Art snoring. He had zoned out, and his rumbling chest was reverberating through her head.

As she lay there, hearing Art snore and thinking about her childhood, an extraordinary thought crossed her mind: *It doesn't have to be that way. Now that I have been set free, I can begin a new story, one that is not moulded by the pain.*

She needed to mull this over. Starting a new story was not something one did lightly, but she at least gave herself permission to explore the possibility as she thought, *Maybe this is what The Great Love has in mind for me.*

Art stopped snoring and opened his eyes, then after giving a very convincing defence that he hadn't been snoring at all, he asked Linda what she was thinking about as she stared off into the distance. They talked at length about the thing that Linda had only ever alluded to before, the pain of losing her mother in such a terrible way, and the suppressed memory of it all that had haunted her ever since. Linda told Art all she could remember about it, how it had affected her over the years, and how The Great Love had set her free by mixing his tears of love with her tears of pain.

Art was more engaged now; he couldn't relate to the river experience, but he empathised with the prison of Linda's pain – and so they began to discuss how one begins a new story. Linda wanted to get it right. She was very aware that her life had been held captive by the pain in her memories and how those memories had twisted every experience and interaction into its own false view of things. This was about much more than simply healing her pain; it was about becoming the person she couldn't be because she had been trapped in her pain – it was about becoming her true self again.

A few carefully chosen words on paper can only go part way to conveying the full scale of the thing Linda was pondering…because it's hard to imagine how a person could have lived their entire life as only a fraction of their true self.

CHAPTER 12
A NEW STORY

The journey to one's true self is not well mapped. There are few sign posts pointing the way, and even fewer people who have actually been there to give directions. Yet it was strangely exhilarating to set out on the journey. Linda was quietly optimistic and even a little eager to get started.

She knew that this was about much more than a bit of fine tuning. Everything about her life had in some way been caught up in the sadness and pain; she had become subconsciously defined by it, and even her attempts to shut it out were in their own way a denial of the truth. In one way or another she had tried to block out the pain over the years, only to find herself back in grief-filled despair before too long – nothing seemed to help, there was no magic formula. So Linda knew that this would involve the complete reconstruction of herself from the ground up – and she was at a complete loss as to how to do that.

She needed help, but who could she turn to?

"Stevie, tell me about the river again; tell me about the Voice and the River of Life. I want to understand what happened in the river – because I think my answers are in there too."

They went through it all again in detail beginning with Eric and Leo all the way to little Linda and her joyful dance. "I think I want what little Linda has," said Linda, "I think the truest version of myself is captured in the spontaneous love dance of little Linda."

As Stevie examined his experience so far, he realised that the Voice spoke to him in two ways: first, at the deepest place inside him, and also in the river – in fact it seemed to be the voice of the River of Life. The River of Life had a voice, and that Voice spoke about The Great Love from whom it all flowed.

Stevie explained this to Linda from the intuitive knowledge that was in his heart. It seemed to come out of him in much the same way that Leo had spoken – that, like Leo, he knew something which was stored in his innermost being, not his intellect. The River of Life did that; it just happened to anyone that lived there.

"I'm sure the Voice can tell you what you need to know, Mum. The Voice knows everything, but especially how the Life flows out from the heart of The Great Love, and how we can get into that flow. I think that's how you will learn about your true self." As I said, for a ten-year-old, that was a lot of information; and it seemed to just tumble out of Stevie's mouth. He didn't really think too much about it…he just knew.

"Why don't you try sitting in your lounge chair and waiting for the Voice to speak?" suggested Stevie.

"Do I have to do anything, Stevie? Is there anything special I need to do to get the Voice to speak?" asked Linda, obviously perplexed.

Stevie thought about that. "I don't think you need to do anything" he said, "I think The Great Love already wants to show you what's next. He just wants you to sit still and receive it – I think he is more interested in your true self than even you are."

So Linda gently brushed Shelley off her chair and sat and waited; nothing seemed to be happening. She tried closing her eyes and opening her eyes, and even closing them a little bit until she could just see through little slits…but nothing. She had been there for half an hour or so and was close to calling it quits when she decided to talk to The Great Love anyway, even though she felt he didn't seem interested in talking to her.

"I don't know who you are, and I don't know what to do" said Linda in a whisper, "but I want you to help me find my true self, the person I was meant to be before the pain took over."

A distant voice began to speak, though not physically distant from Linda because it was inside her. It was distant because it was speaking from the river within the river, and Linda was unfamiliar with that place, and even more unfamiliar with hearing from it. It was like a voice speaking to Linda from across the ages and expanses of history, speaking from another realm entirely, and inviting Linda to open herself up to a new way of communing – heart to heart instead of head to head.

"I don't know how to communicate with my heart," Linda half thought and half whispered. "Yes, you do," assured the Voice, "it's just that you haven't done it for a very long time. If you like, I will help you to learn all over again."

And so began Linda's re-education in the ways of the heart.

"Communicating by the heart is very ancient, yet very immediate," said the Voice. "You were designed by The Great Love to commune with him just as he communes with all created beings – by the unforced rhythms of love. It is the language he speaks – in fact, it is the only language he speaks – and all who wish to speak with him must learn it. The love you have known all your life is just a shadow of true love; it is the superficial love of the visible river and barely touches the real thing. When you know true love, you will know your true self."

'Stunned' would best describe Linda's reaction. *I don't understand what any of that means,* she thought, *it's like a completely different way to be, a completely new existence, and I have no idea where to begin.*

"Yes," said the Voice, "if you are not stunned, then you are missing something, because this new self bears little resemblance to the self you have known all your life. You can't simply change your language and the outwardly visible things like your behaviour and attitudes; they are nothing more than the visible expression of who you really are inside. It is necessary to actually be changed into someone completely different and new, someone who hasn't existed for a very, very long time."

"And you have no capacity within yourself to do this."

"Then how can this happen?" asked Linda. "How can I become my true self if I have no capacity to change myself?"

"The answer is simple" said the Voice. "The Great Love will change you if you trust him, but he cannot change you if you remain attached to who you were; he can only do it if you let go and trust him."

"But why do I need to change who I am? Why can't I just get my pain removed?"

At last, Linda was at the nub of the thing…the question she asked had drilled down to the very heart of her problem – the very essence of her being.

"You need to be changed back into your true design because, although you cannot see it, you barely resemble the person you were created to be when The Great Love conceived you as the overflow of his love. Life on earth has laid claim to you and remade you into its own broken image – that's why you don't just need to be patched up; you need to be reborn."

The Voice spoke volumes into Linda's heart, describing the journey she was confronting. "The Great Love knows you better than you know yourself, but the 'you' he knows is the true you. You don't know your true self; you still think it is merely an improved version of the person you have always known. But, Linda, it is not. These two people are as different as night and day, as different even as death and life. You cannot hurry this process, or jump into it casually, because it marks the end of your life as you have known it."

"It cannot begin yet, because you have yet to let go; and you need some time of reflection for that to happen." With that, the Voice stopped talking. The deepest part of Linda knew there was nothing more to be said today – she would give it time.

Linda wanted a new story, one that wasn't influenced and directed by her past sadness and pain, but she wasn't sure she was ready to end the life she had always known – she wasn't even sure what that meant. But she had time on her side. The week was just beginning, and the family would be busy with their lives; there would be plenty of opportunity for reflection.

A new story, she mused. *I guess I can't start a new story unless I become a new person.* The old person will continue to write the same old story, the pain and sadness might be gone but the person who received that brokenness is still there. *But who would I become, do I really want to be someone else, someone I don't even know – and dare I let him do it?*

CHAPTER 13
A NEW PERSON

The week rolled by slowly.

Linda contemplated all that had happened so far. Each day she found time to sit quietly and reflect on the things the Voice had said. She didn't arrive at any conclusions, but she knew in her heart that everything was on track; it would all fall into place in its own time.

She decided to join Stevie at the river again on Saturday and see if the environment of the river could provide her with any new insights.

They set off together again just like the previous week, except this time they didn't hold hands because Stevie was not grounded anymore, so he had a lot of things to carry. Linda brought along a few deck chairs to make it a little more comfortable and a small basket of food to get them through the long day out.

This was not a Saturday like the previous ones where the river surprised Stevie and Linda with strange voices and experiences; the river was just a river – to be enjoyed and observed, and especially to be fished. There was no thought of Eric and Leo; they didn't even cross Stevie's mind, the river was simply the place Stevie loved, and he allowed it to fill his senses and captivate him in the way it always had.

So naturally, he began to fish, and he drifted into the easy pace of it all. Fishing is an unhurried thing; you just go with it. You just bait up and cast the line and wait. Stevie fished as if none of the previous two Saturdays had even happened, and he began to catch fish too.

First a nice little cod decided to take the bait, and Stevie enjoyed reeling it in and holding it. Once it was on shore, Stevie removed the hook and looked it over. "What do you think, Mum, is it a bit small?" Linda nodded her agreement, so Stevie gently placed the fish back in the water.

The time passed slowly, but neither Stevie or Linda cared. This was a very nice place to be spending a slow day, and they both fell into an easy rhythm of sitting, and talking, and silence.

Sometime later, a much bigger fish took the bait; it was a bream – the tastiest of all river fish – and Stevie was determined to land it. This one didn't give in so easily, and whenever the fish made a dash for it, Stevie had to give it some room to move so that it didn't break the line, and then slowly reel it back in again. After ten minutes, Stevie was tiring, but so was the fish. Linda gave the occasional encouragement, but mostly she just sat back and watched her son do the thing he loved most. Eventually they could see the fish just meters away, and what a beauty it was! Stevie really wanted that fish, but just as he was about to place his net under it, the fish gave one final frenzied flip of its tail – the line was broken, and the big fish swam off as casually as could be.

Stevie was torn between the exhilaration of the battle and the ultimate let-down of losing the catch, and Linda watched to see how he would deal with it. He responded by sitting and staring into the water in front of him; he relived the moment in his mind and then let the tension of the fight slowly recede from his body. Then he looked over to Linda and smiled as he remarked thoughtfully, "The big ones are really hard to land."

They shared a sandwich and a drink and relaxed for a bit before Stevie baited up again.

Before long, Stevie had cast out again and settled onto his seat to play the waiting game. He had the right disposition for this; his was alert yet patient, the perfect combination. And it paid off soon enough as he felt the tug on his line. *Another big one,* thought Stevie. The same sort of battle transpired, with Stevie playing out the line then reeling it back in, hoping this time he would be the victor. Once again the fish appeared within sight, breaking the surface occasionally as it fought the line, but unable to elude its grip. Stevie had it in the shallows.

"Grab the net, Mum" he yelled, then he hoisted the fish out of the water while Linda scooped it up – a beautiful silver perch, Stevie beamed. He had caught big fish before, but never with his mum watching on; this was a great day indeed for Stevie – a two-kilogram perch.

After that, the day was considered a success, so Linda sat back comfortably into the deck chair and enjoyed the fresh air and sunshine, leaving Stevie to his fishing without her watchful gaze. Stevie repeated his routine of success and failure – it was all part of fishing – but Linda was lost in her own thoughts.

She thought about the river…its captivating beauty and serenity. She thought about the living things in the river and the diverse system of life that existed beneath the surface, and she thought about the river within the river – what exactly is it?

She silently whispered to the Voice, "Can you explain the river within the river?"

Deep inside her the Voice said, "I can explain it in words, or I can show you."

That put Linda on the spot. She hadn't exactly prepared herself for a guided tour; she was thinking that an impression or a thought process might be provided, but a guided tour was way out there. And she didn't know if she had sufficiently contemplated the whole thing yet; the idea of 'letting go' was still just a vague concept.

"You will never be completely ready," commented the Voice. "Your intellect is too attached to the natural realm and will always be in conflict with your heart…trust me?"

That was Linda's problem. She couldn't find a way to rationalize this, and it didn't fit into any box that contained her neatly arranged thought processes and experiences. Yet something more real and compelling than rational thinking pulled at her. She knew this was what she needed to do because her heart was slowly and gently moving her forward…so she listened to her heart.

Linda rested her head back, closed her eyes and gave the Voice permission to show her the river within the river.

She felt herself floating, leaving herself behind and looking down at things from a great height.

First the voice showed her the natural river and how it worked. See how Stevie stares at the river and tries to understand it and all that is happening in it? See how he works at catching fish and pulling them in with all his effort and ingenuity? See how he does all of this from the river bank? This is how life works in your world – all human beings are fishing for something, trying to get it onto dry land…and most of all, they are fishing for love.

"My world is different," said the Voice. "We do not fish."

Then the Voice told her to close her eyes and look with her heart. "Look at the same scene with your inner sight; trust yourself to see deeper into the river where the Life is at work."

The Voice went on to explain that there is another world within the world (a river within the river), but it cannot be perceived with our natural senses. Still, in spite of that, it is even more real and tangible than the visible river.

So Linda closed her eyes and relaxed her instinct to perceive things with her senses…and waited. She switched off all her in-built connections that reported to her their continuous newsreel of the physical information going on around her, and she allowed her inner self to take over.

The river faded…it became opaque and indistinct; it was nothing more than a visible shell that held the real thing, and as Linda continued to look with the eyes of her heart, the river became less and less in focus. There was another world in there, hidden much deeper inside it; it had simply been obscured by all the information reported to her by her natural sight.

This world was tangible not because it contained physical objects, because it was not a world of physical things

– yet somehow it contained a reality far beyond things. It was indeed a river because it flowed, beginning at its source, The Great Love, and flowing relentlessly over and through everything in its path; it was unstoppable and uncontainable – such was the nature of The Great Love which was its source.

Powerful, yet tender – raging, yet sweet – overwhelming, yet liberating; the River of Life flowed out from The Great Love. It reached into every crevice…every hidden space was filled, and every living creature was saturated in its relentless obsession to give love.

Linda looked further in; she could see the scale and might of the river – but she was powerfully drawn to the love.

"Why can't I see the love more clearly?" she asked the Voice longingly, "I want to let it hold me; I want to be washed by it." The Voice replied with great tenderness, "When you let go, it will fill you. It is not being held back by The Great Love; it is being held back by you."

With that, Linda found herself back in her deck chair. The River of Life had disappeared, and the river Hopkins flowed slowly on before her. But she had seen the river within the river – deep inside her she had seen it – and she knew she could never be the same again. In fact, nothing could be the same again. She had seen enough and understood enough to make her decision.

Linda had been around the Christian faith for her whole life, and she recognised the concept of the Kingdom of God which existed beyond the natural realm. But the River of Life seemed to be different. It was another realm altogether which contained the natural realm. It was not beyond it…it held it; and it was asking her to entrust her entire existence into its care. *The natural realm clamours for my attention,* she thought. *It tells me to fish from it – but I was designed by The Great Love to rest in the flow of his life, not fish from the banks in the hope of catching his life by my own self-effort.*

CHAPTER 14
THE DECISION

Linda made her decision: she decided to be a person who dwelt in the River of Life. She decided to let go.

But no sooner had she made the decision than she doubted herself. Making the decision was the easy part; she knew in her heart that it was the most obvious course to take, but entrusting herself and her whole life to that decision was another thing altogether. Her problem was not that she didn't want the River of Life. She just wasn't sure that she was ready to give her entire existence into it – and what would be left of her, and all of the things that made up her life, if she did.

It was another quiet afternoon at home with her and Stevie in the kitchen together, which was becoming more and more the way things went. They seemed to gravitate to the same space more often than before, not by plan or even request – it just seemed to happen without much thought, Linda at the sink preparing something, and Stevie at the table doing…not much.

"Stevie, tell me about the talking fish. You said something about Eric and Lennie?"

"Leo, Mum – Eric and Leo."

"They seemed to be different from each other" questioned Linda, "Eric lived in the Hopkins River but was oblivious to the River of Life that flowed within it, but Leo seemed to know all about the river within the river, he seemed to know something – is that right?"

"Hmmm, yes – Eric laughed at Leo when he spoke about it."

"I wonder why Eric didn't understand?" said Linda, "You would think that if he lived in it, he would want to learn how to trust it?"

"Eric isn't very smart Mum – I don't think he thinks about anything much. He just lives and lets the river flow without much thought; he talks a lot, but when you get right down to it, he lives on the edge, and his life just happens."

"But Leo is another fish altogether; he knows something…" Stevie couldn't put into words exactly what it was that Leo knew or even how knowing it made any difference – he just knew it did.

"What's going on, Mum? Why are we talking about this?"

Linda thought about that. She was thirty-eight and Stevie was ten – this could all sound a bit odd, and it might come out all wrong. Linda wasn't sure that Stevie was old enough to understand what it was like to reflect on life and make a decision to change half way through – she wasn't even sure she understood herself – that's why she was asking all the questions.

Linda launched in. "I think I've been living like Eric, and I want to live like Leo. I don't want to be like Eric, but I think I am because life just happens to me – I want to be like Leo, I want to live because I know something…"

There it was again, the mysterious 'something' – what exactly was it?

"What do you think Leo knows?" queried Linda.

"Maybe you need to ask the Voice," replied Stevie, handing to Linda what had become his standard reply lately.

Linda looked intently toward Stevie – but she was really looking beyond him to what he had said. Then, without hesitation, she walked into the lounge room and sat down in her armchair, closed her eyes and let the day's distractions fall away as she asked the Voice to tell her what the 'something' was that she needed to know. Slowly, her inner self began to emerge, and a dialogue of hearts opened up to her.

"You have decided to let go," said the Voice, "and that is good. You have decided to let go of the props that have held your life in place to this point, but now you must also take hold of the new, in place of the old – and you are uncertain about what the new is, so doubts creep in."

Linda knew this was true; she was well aware of the unstable foundation upon which her life was built and knew that she needed that to change, but she didn't know enough about The Great Love to completely entrust herself into his care. She knew she felt good whenever she was close to The Great Love, but she didn't know if The Great Love was able to hold her life in the way that her past had held it. It all came down to the fact that she didn't know if love could or would actually carry her any better than her pain had.

"There is 'letting go' and there is 'taking hold' – and you need to do both," encouraged the Voice. "The Great

Love has got you either way, but it is important that you have also got The Great Love."

"Think about Eric; the River of Life flows all around him, but he has no idea that it is happening, so he lives his life without certainty – he just exists."

"And think about Leo; he is held in place by the River of Life, and because he knows it and rests in the certainty of it, he is able to live without fear – so he doesn't just exist, he lives. Even though Leo remains in the Hopkins River, he lives with great confidence and peace because he knows that The Great Love has got him. Leo has let go of the Hopkins River as the source of his life and taken hold of living in the River of Life; he knows that The Great Love can be trusted…with everything."

That is the thing Leo knows.

Linda was becoming confused. She understood with her heart, but her head still didn't get it. It was like two realities existed in parallel, and Linda couldn't see them clearly enough to separate them. Her head wanted to simply improve her existence in the natural realm, and her heart wanted to escape the natural realm altogether and relocate to the River of Life.

Her head wanted to fish from the River of Life from the safety of the firm ground in the natural realm. It wanted to secure all the good things contained in the River of Life while maintaining her security in the visible realm – and her heart wanted to escape altogether and cross over into the other realm.

"It all comes down to the source from which you live, and consequently your relationship to that source," explained the Voice. "Some people are unaware that The

Great Love even exists, and they just live; some people are aware that he exists and simply want him to help them by putting things on the hook they dangle in front of him. Still others are aware that he exists but are too attached to the realm of nature, so they remake him into an extension of themselves. Finally, a very few are aware he exists and that his heart is full of great love for them, and so they relocate their existence into the care of that great love forever.

"Those who make that relocation are effectively residents of another realm; though they remain physically in the realm of nature, their true existence is found in the River of Life, so their lives are continuously held and nurtured by the source of life in the realm in which they live.

"There is nothing wrong with living in the realm of nature; it was The Great Love's gift to you when he created you – but you weren't designed to be defined by it or find your life source in it. For that, only the River of Life will do. All of humankind was made for the River of Life, and yet most of humanity has chosen the natural realm to provide for their sense of self and wellbeing.

"They think they can gain the things of the heart, which flow only from The Great Love, through the means of the self-effort which defines the natural realm."

The Voice was speaking in sweeping terms of the problem with human beings. His words were more than mere human contemplation…more even than deep philosophy. He was trying to get Linda's resistant mind to grasp an idea which was so completely abstract to her ingrained thinking that the stubborn obstruction in her might finally be broken down by his many words.

On and on he spoke, "People don't understand what is wrong with them. They think they need a better life in the natural realm, but that is only a small fraction of their true self. They really need to stop trying to fix their natural lives by attracting The Great Love's attention; instead, they need to relocate themselves permanently into him and his love – that is where the true self is found. Most people live their lives as if 'things' are transferable between the two realms, but that is not true; only Life can be transferred between realms."

Linda could sense that the Voice was coming to the end of his lengthy discourse, that he had laid his foundation and had only one final thing to add. Something big was coming…she could sense it, like all of eternity held its breath and then in one great sigh the truth was laid bare for Linda to see…the heart of The Great Love exposed in one short sentence.

"Linda, if you want to truly take possession of The Great Love, you must die."

The world stood still; eternity, nature and the existence of all living things were suspended in that one sentence. No one breathed, not a living creature moved, the stars and planets held their position in the universe while Linda absorbed this truth – the great crossing was taking place and the entire creation knew it and stared in wonder at the marvel of it – the crossing from death to life.

You see, so few people cross over anymore; most live in a hybrid existence of their own making, a blending of the two worlds – but so few perceive the truth that living with a foot in each world is really only choosing the lesser one, and so they never fully step from the old existence across to the new. However, when this does take place, the universe takes notice; everything holds its breath in anticipation of the extraordinary event taking place before their eyes – it is one of the greatest spectacles ever seen in the invisible realm, because it is the birth of a brand new invisible heart.

It is one thing to be loved by The Great Love, but to entrust oneself completely into that love is another thing altogether – and Linda stood on the cusp of her rebirth.

She leaned over the edge, as it were, and then in her heart she stepped out and her old life fell away like an old discarded garment that had had its day.

She was soaring now, carried aloft by a new energy beyond herself, graceful yet carefree she soared through all the days that had numbered humanity, soaring out through the limits that had bookended the realm of time – and then she saw eternity before her far more expansive and greater than the limits of human history, shining in all its glory and bursting with divine life, and she pierced it and was in – and the love that filled her being was heavier than an ocean, yet as light as the mist that rose up from the river.

In an instant she knew she was home; this was her birth place, the place where her true self was formed by the unrestrained creative expression of The Great Love – and she saw him too, and wept with joy for the extravagance of it all. She saw him according to his true nature, not according to any physical form she had ever imagined or been taught, and she saw that he was profoundly good and that love flowed relentlessly from his heart like a mighty river – and in seeing him…she became like him.

CHAPTER 15
AWAKENING

Linda awoke as if from an ecstatic dream; she was back home in her lounge room…but not. The environment around her was the same as when she closed her eyes, but there was something different about it – that something was 'Life', her existence had a strange new kind of life in it. There was a dynamic all around her that hadn't been there when she sat down – she had brought eternity back with her.

This new dynamic, indeed this new life, was not visible to the human eye. It had no physical evidence to mark its existence; the only reason Linda could see it was that the eyes of her heart were seeing things clearly now. She could see with her heart, and what she saw was the presence of an all-pervading love expressing itself through a new vital, urgent kind of life. Yet this new life was not new at all; it had been there all along, just as the River of Life was there all along. It just couldn't be seen by those who made the home of their heart in the natural realm.

It is a very strange sensation to be in a world within a world for the first time. Things that seemed so tangible before lose some of their substance as the Life that holds them in place becomes clearer. It is the Life now that has substance, and the things are secondary and having little relevance apart from it. Ordinary objects in the room had taken on a new dynamic; Linda could see how they held together – not their molecular structure or the quantum physics that held them together, but the life force that gave their molecular structure its substance… the Life that flows from the heart of The Great Love.

Linda was no geophysicist, she had no training in any scientific discipline at all, in fact she only completed high school and never went on to further study; nevertheless, she could see that all this existed outside of the laws of science and could not be explained by them. It was bigger than science because it gave to science and nature the one thing it needed to exist – the selfless life-giving dynamic that can only come from outside itself…divine love.

This love force that held the universe and all it contained in place resonated in Linda's heart – she had become a part of it when she went home to her true origins. You see, in discovering her true self, she had become of the same nature as her maker.

Linda knew this instinctively. She knew it better than she knew her own face. She had died and been reborn as the true self The Great Love had in mind when he first conceived her in eternity, and she somehow knew it with every fibre of her being – it had become registered so deep with her that it was now the all-pervading fact of her existence.

Stevie came into the room. As soon as he saw his mother's face, he asked "Mum, what happened?" There was a lot Linda could have answered, but instead she asked, "What do you mean, Stevie?"

"Well," responded Stevie thoughtfully, "You look sort of new. Something is radiating from inside you that wasn't there before – you kind of remind me of little Linda."

His mum smiled her big smile, and Stevie smiled his as he hopped up into her lap and bathed in the joy of it. He kept looking at Linda, as if trying to see inside her, and Linda laughed at him with such unrestrained happiness that they both fell off the chair and lay flat out on the floor with unrestrained wild laughter and giggling – something else that hadn't happened for a very long time.

That was the moment that Art chose to arrive home from work. He came in the back door and heard the wild laughter and stealthily crept up to look, and as he peeped his head around the corner, he saw something that took his breath away…Linda had become beautiful.

She was by far the most beautiful woman he had ever seen.

On closer inspection, he could see that she was the same person he had kissed goodbye when he left for work that morning, but she now possessed an inner radiance that wasn't there when he had left. Linda had become beautiful on the inside, and it radiated all the way through her so that she appeared beautiful on the outside too. It wasn't the beauty of celebrities and models, but a completely pure and innocent beauty that reflected her true self.

This wasn't something that Linda had bargained on; she had no expectation that her true self would impact her outward appearance; but such is the nature of The Great Love – he is so surprisingly extravagant.

Art continued to stare at Linda with a goofy look on his face.

"What?" questioned Linda.

Art groped for words and eventually came up with, "You have always been lovely to me. You took my breath away on our wedding day eighteen years ago, and you just did it again when I walked into the room. It's like I am seeing you for the first time all over again, only this time it's even more breath-taking. Something very beautiful is shining out of your face." And with that, Art blushed and smiled bashfully.

The Voice spoke to Linda's heart: "You have become one with The Great Love. Your new self must now learn how to live as this new person. Today you begin the adventure of living as the person The Great Love imagined you to be in the beginning – the real Linda is on display for the world to see, and you have been set free to be her. Go and love being your true self."

It was all happening – both of Linda's worlds were connecting with her; both were full on. The big difference was that she was now engaged with the natural realm as a person whose identity was held firmly by the River of Life.

Linda had wondered what would happen to her life in the natural realm once she had relocated herself to the River of Life. She'd had no way of knowing beforehand, but now she got it. First she had to become her true self, and once that had happened, the life that flowed out of The Great Love flowed spontaneously out of her – she really had become like him.

It is all about discovering the truth as The Great Love sees it and allowing that truth to have you – all of you, she thought. It couldn't happen until Linda completely entrusted herself into the care of The Great Love; otherwise it would have been like a cocktail of two sources of life – which of course ultimately leads to the lower source taking charge.

Art had settled down by this time, but he and Stevie still exchanged bewildered glances, so Linda chimed in, "Look, guys, this is new for all of us; I'm still getting used to it too. So let's give it a few days, and then I will try to answer your questions." Art and Stevie nodded dumbly.

Linda had never seen them like this. They had never been short of words before, but here they were behaving like two boys on their first day at kindergarten when their pretty young teacher first enters the room. She decided it was time to see for herself, so she casually excused herself and went to check herself out in the bathroom mirror.

Nothing – there was no discernible change.

She saw only those annoying grey hairs still trying to assert themselves, and those early mid-life wrinkles still around her mouth and eyes. Nose a bit too big, eyes too far apart.

As Linda turned away from the mirror, she caught a fleeting image of herself. "Wait a minute, that wasn't there yesterday; I would have noticed." – but it was there! It was like she had a twin sister who was looking back at her, but this person had something Linda had never possessed: she radiated a contented poise and a gentle confidence that comes only from being deeply and unconditionally loved. Then Linda looked back and studied herself again with the eyes of her heart, and she saw what the others had seen – The Great Love was looking back at her in human form.

The old Linda had indeed died and been reborn of Love; her reflection made that plain – this was the true self that she was now free to be, and she didn't even have to try. All she had to do was entrust herself to The Great Love, and he would live his life through her. Others would simply see the radiant beauty of The Great Love within her.

"The River of Life will do this," assured the Voice. "It is his part to play; it is what he does."

Excitement, anticipation, exhilaration – all of these filled Linda. She felt she could simply burst with wonder and anticipation at what lay ahead for her and the new colour in her life she so desired, and at the same time she rested fully confident that it would happen because of the new life in her, not because of her own self-effort.

That's the difference, thought Linda – *my life is now carried along by the flow that originates at the divine source; it is The Great Love's life in me that will bring all this to pass.*

Linda thought of Kate who was staying with friends for the night. *What will she think?* But it was enough for one day. She bid the boys goodnight and collapsed into a deep sleep. She wasn't so much exhausted…more like overwhelmed. Living with The Great Love had that effect on her – it was like a state of constant readiness. The flow was always there, pulling at her and drawing her into its constant movement. She needed a lot of sleep to carry such an intense vitality of love that was always on stand-by.

And as Linda slept, Art sat and pondered things.

Their marriage had always been the anchor in his life – perhaps not so much in the overtly expressive sense, but more like an atmosphere that had settled around him and seemed to fit him very comfortably. Over the years, he and Linda had shaped themselves around each other. Their personalities and individuality giving way to an easy blending of their more retiring natures, which resulted in a sense of being more defined by their togetherness than their independence. They had become one – two shy people who had found each other, and it seemed to him that a single complete person had grown out of the union.

But now one of them was changing, and Art wondered what that meant for them…for him. The changes in Stevie were more easily dismissed as the overflow of his frequent lapsings into the world of daydream – but Linda was not like Stevie in that way; she was consistent and dependable – the glue that held the family in place – and he didn't want the familiar fabric of his life to become unstuck.

In short, Art didn't know how to be anyone else, and the thought of changing the balance of things unsettled him. As much as the change in Linda excited him, it also caused him to feel strangely vulnerable. You see, the appearance of the new beautiful Linda seemed to bring with it a completeness in her that Art felt he could not match – their relationship had always been strong because in their mutual shyness they held on tightly to each other for support…but he wondered if the new Linda would still need that.

Yet his anxiety was mingled with a tender anticipation that the thing that was happening in Linda was good – good for them both – and he quieted himself and his fears with the hope that he was right.

Eventually Art went to bed. He crept in quietly and eased into bed, attempting his best to not disturb Linda; but she moved a little as he nestled in, and they settled into their familiar spaces in the bed – Art facing away from Linda in case he snored, and Linda maintaining contact with her hand on his back. This was the way they had slept for years, and it fitted them like a glove and seemed to enable sleep to come easily to them both, and so it was that night. Art pondered that evening's events for a little while, but before long sleep overtook him, and he relaxed into a sleep so deep that he was barely breathing. As they slept in this way, Art began to dream, but not a dream that came from the day's events or the temperature of his body; it was a dream that flowed out of Linda's hand on his back and directly into his heart.

Art began to dream out of Linda's new reality.

He dreamt he was in a wide river, swimming across it to reach his family on the other side. He loved to swim and was glad they lived so close to the river. His wiry frame and the physicality of his work had crafted him into the ideal swimmer's physique, and it was the one activity that he felt most agreed with him. At first, he swam easily and strongly and found himself stroking the water in a confident rhythm. As he neared the middle of the river, he felt the current pull at him, but this did not alarm Art; he had felt it many times before as he swam across the river. His usual practice was to think of the faces of his family and swim toward them; it always gave him the extra strength he needed to overcome the pull of the current. But this time was different. Art felt his arms tire and his legs weaken and the current began to win – he began to drift away from his family instead of getting closer.

Strangely, he didn't panic. For some inexplicable reason, Art knew everything would be okay; he just slowed his pace and swam more gently in a way that didn't tax his energy so much and let the current take him. He swam for a very long time, ever so gradually edging closer to the far river bank, which changed in appearance as he was carried along around the river bends and straights. His family were lost from view by now; they were miles back. Yet still he swam on to reach the side, thinking he could walk back to them once he had rested on the bank for a short while.

But his progress was so slow and his effort so unrewarded that he began to wonder if he would ever get there, and even though he was making some progress, the river was also getting wider as it went along so that his gains amounted to very little. The minutes turned into hours and then even days as Art swam; all he could do was swim and hope. He had lost complete sense of time and control of the outcome. He was totally at the mercy of the river…and this river didn't show much mercy.

After swimming for a very, very long time Art had had enough. The point of it all was lost, and he came to the realisation that he was just swimming without any real chance of ever reaching the other side, and he didn't know what to do. He considered stopping and letting the river carry him wherever it wanted, but he had never been a quitter and his family needed him – so he swam on.

Art lost track of all time and conscious thought, he had just become a swimming machine, not really a person, just a swimmer who had no choice but to swim.

Then, seemingly out of nowhere, Art bumped into something…well, it was actually someone, someone else swimming across the river in the other direction. Art didn't know the guy; he was just a stranger, and they both stopped to talk while treading water.

"How are you getting on?" asked Art.

"Great," said the mysterious swimmer, "this is my third crossing today."

"But aren't you finding the current difficult? How do you manage it? I'm completely done in."

"I'm not surprised," responded the mysterious swimmer. "You're in the wrong river." And he winked at Art before swimming off at such a pace that Art could only stare in disbelief.

Then Art bumped into something else, the river bank – he had reached the other side and his family were relaxing on the bank while they waited for him to come ashore. "Hi, Dad," greeted Stevie. "Good swim?"

Art just towelled himself dry and nodded, still trying to make out what had just happened.

"I'm in the wrong river – what a strange thing to say."

CHAPTER 16

DREAMS

Art and Linda woke earlier than usual, so they made the most of the extra time and enjoyed a coffee and toast in bed before the morning rush.

"I dreamt the strangest dream last night, Linda," said Art, remembering it in vivid detail.

"I'm usually the one that bores you with my dreams," said Linda, "so it's your turn – tell me all about it."

Art related his dream to Linda from start to finish… all of the details and even the emotions he felt about not being able to make any headway. "And then I bumped into another swimmer who said I was in the wrong river, to cap it all off. And then I arrived at the other side of the river without even trying – very strange dream."

Linda knew in her heart this was not the time to comment; she would know when to say something.

"What are you going to be doing today, honey?" she asked instead.

"Same old, same old," replied Art, "Just loading and unloading timber onto trucks…" – then musing almost as if to himself, "…just like a swimmer who has no choice but to swim." Not that he was complaining, this was just his lot in life…but the dream had unsettled something in him.

Art didn't hate his job, but he didn't love it either. He was just neutral about it. He had been doing it for so long now that it had become like walking with a limp; it was just part of him. People who limp might be glad to be walking, but they would rather run, or at least jog. That was Art's life; he went to work five days a week and brought home the income needed to support his family, with nothing left over for extras. He was a good man who did an honest day's work – but there was no real joy in it.

Linda kissed him and, on impulse, told him how much she loved him and appreciated his hard work for the family – and that was enough for Art to get over his melancholy. He picked himself up and got into his work clothes for another day of being just another cog in the machine.

As he was dressing, he looked over at Linda and was stunned once again by the beauty radiating from her. "Wow, you look gorgeous," he told her, and when Linda grinned back at him, he knew that somehow this was all going to turn out.

He knew something good was happening to his family, and he had a feeling he was next in line, yet his musings as he had sat alone the previous evening continued to play in his mind as he wondered again, *How can I keep in step with such a beautiful transformation?*

His thoughts seesawed between wonder and despair. The faint hope of a life less controlled by work and obligations pulled at him, as though a part of him that had long ago been buried by the expectations of life had been spoken to by love, and it wanted to respond. And the thought that he also could be caught up in Linda's transformation wooed him in the strangest way and made suggestions to his stoic endurance that the day of his blessed release was near.

As Art was cleaning up in the kitchen, Stevie wandered in. "I had the strangest dream about you last night, Dad," he said as they passed each other.

"Sit down and tell me about it while I get you some breakfast."

So Stevie related his dream to Art, and it was word for word the same dream that Art had…except for one thing. The stranger didn't say, "You're in the wrong river." Instead, he said, "It isn't what you think it is," just like the Voice had said to Stevie a few weeks earlier.

"Are you sure he said that?" asked Art. "Are you sure you haven't forgotten and just made that last bit up?"

"Nope, that's what he said; and then he winked and swam off at a hundred miles an hour" ended Stevie confidently.

That was the same dream all right, so maybe the message from the stranger was the same message, only worded differently.

It isn't what you think it is – very strange indeed.

Art knew that Stevie was inclined to daydream; he knew that Stevie had a pretend world inside his head that covered a lot of things pertaining to the river and fishing, but this was far too coincidental to be ignored. So he packed it away in his head to be thought about later when he had a free moment at work.

As it turned out, Art didn't get a free moment to think at work. It was all go from start to finish – trucks were lined up to be loaded and unloaded two and three deep, and he even had lunch on the run. He arrived home at six that night, much later than his usual time, tired and grumpy from such a hard day's work.

Linda picked up on his mood and put a beer in front of him as soon as he entered the kitchen. As Art sipped his beer, Linda came around behind him and gently massaged his head and neck. "Nice," murmured Art, and the hectic day fell away to be replaced by a deep sense of peace. As Linda eased the tension out of his neck with her gentle touch, Art shut his eyes and went with it, and he was instantly in the river again – stroking his way through life and getting nowhere.

"Your touch has the weirdest effect on me," muttered Art, obviously puzzled. "It takes me to places I thought I had closed the door on."

"How do you mean, Art, what places? Why are they closed?" After sitting and thinking for a few minutes, Art began to explain to Linda the thoughts that were simmering beneath his nonchalant surface.

Art spoke of his father, and how he felt like he was becoming him, and how his father's mantra of hard work and low personal expectations had shaped him into who he was today. "It's like my dad is sitting on my shoulder directing my life, deciding for me what is important and what my next move should be." He explained that his dad was a good guy who he loved, but life had been hard for his family and times had been difficult. So, Art had grown up in an environment that was more characterised by stoic determination than outward happiness. "I've been working at the same job since I was eighteen, Linda, and it has numbed me – I've lost the ability to choose, and even the confidence to know if I have the right to."

Now that he had lifted the lid off his feelings, Art could see inside himself with some clarity. He hadn't looked in there for a long time because his ingrained work ethic and self-depreciation had kept that door closed. Even now, he felt self-indulgent and childish for turning the spotlight on to himself. "Ah, its' nothing, Linda. I'll get over it – a warm meal and a good sleep and tomorrow will be fine."

But Linda wouldn't have it. She had never heard her husband talk like this, and she wasn't about to let him close the lid back on it again so soon. She kissed him on the head and said, "Art Linden, you are a good man who deserves better. I know you don't get introspective very often, and you don't particularly like doing it, but this is important."

And then like a light bulb was switched on, Linda understood something. "Art, your love and respect for your dad is not compromised if you choose your own path – these are different matters altogether. It may be that when you were eighteen you needed some direction and your dad gave you a push, but now that is past and your dad's memory will not be insulted if you begin to think your own thoughts instead of his."

Art didn't normally think this deeply; it wasn't something guys like him did, but there was a ring of truth to all this, and even a strange tingle of excitement as to what it might mean.

"There is a security in my familiar life, Linda; it seems to have settled on me for so long now that I don't know if I could do things differently…or be different. I know who I am right now, and while it is boring and unfulfilling, I have become entrenched and comfortable with myself – I'm not sure that I'm game to change."

"Well, there's no hurry," Linda assured him as she got back to preparing dinner, "but we have started something just now, and I won't let it drop. Let's pick it up again later when the kids are in bed."

By eight thirty, the house was quiet, Stevie in bed asleep and Kate in bed reading.

"What would you do if you had your time over?" asked Linda, looking directly into his eyes. "If you didn't feel compelled to follow your dad's lead, what would you have done differently?"

Art was not outwardly a big personality; he was shy and a bit insular like Stevie. His appearance matched his personality, and though he was above average height, he unconsciously stooped a little so as not to stand out. The only thing he couldn't hide was his mop of hair that seemed to grow quicker than Linda could cut it, and so his retreat into obscurity was never quite complete.

"For a start, I'm not unhappy. You need to know that – I am content in our life together. And I haven't really indulged in this kind of thing before, so it's not that close to the surface; but I think I would have liked to go to university and get a degree instead of going straight into a job after leaving high school."

"What kind of degree?" questioned Linda, fascinated by the conversation they were having and amazed that she hadn't picked up on it before.

"I will tell you as long as you promise not to laugh," agreed Art, and Linda promised.

Art was embarrassed and awkward about opening up the subject, but also just a little bit exhilarated to expose his boyhood dream to Linda. "I always thought I could be a teacher," he stated rather uncertainly, and Linda just stared at him, her eyes wide.

"Really, Art, you really wanted to be a teacher? You could so have been a teacher, Art, you would be the best at it. Why did you think I would laugh?"

"I thought you might laugh at me for having such a high opinion of myself; I thought you might find it amusing that a fork-lift driver thinks he could be a teacher."

"What would you have liked to teach, Art? What subjects appeal to you that you would like to teach?"

"I think I would have liked to teach English and history," replied Art. "I found those subjects really caught hold of me in high school; they really meant something to me."

"I am going to make an observation, and you correct me if I'm wrong," said Linda cautiously. "You hardly pick up a book, Art, and we hardly ever talk about history or literature. I think that is because you let your dream die – you have deliberately avoided those things, in fact you culled them from your life because you felt your dream to be a teacher was lost to you. Is that right?"

Art nodded.

"I just couldn't bear reading beautiful or thought-provoking books anymore. I couldn't bring myself to love history because I thought my path was set, and there was no use pretending. You're right, Honey, I died to my dream…but now I'm beginning to wonder if my dream died to me, I think it's still in there after all these years."

"Funny thing is, Art, that all of this crazy and wonderful stuff we are going through right now began with Stevie who is the ultimate daydreamer. There is something very important in having a dream; it is like a gift from your heart, and I think we have to get you your dream back."

As those words came out of Linda's mouth, Art immediately thought of the words from his and Stevie's dreams: *You're in the wrong river – it isn't what you think it is.*

CHAPTER 17

CHANGING YOUR MIND

Art and Linda talked long into the night.

They talked about growing up and what their lives had looked like when they were younger and their future together that still lay ahead of them. They talked about how they felt then and how they feel now, and all the stuff that life had handed to them which ultimately formed them into themselves. And of course they talked about their dreams and hopes, and all the things that had filled their heads when they were much younger which seemed to have faded from view since. They laughed at some things, like falling in love so young and how they felt about each other as children, and were both very grateful to have each other in spite of all that life had handed them.

They both concluded that life had a way of trapping people, that it exerted its influence and pulled people into a version of themselves that was like a type of prison – they were held captive by all the stuff that landed on them and were stuck there, unable to help themselves or escape from it all.

Linda didn't say much about The Great Love yet; she knew the time was coming soon, but she didn't want to run ahead of the Voice and spoil it for Art. She knew it would happen when The Great Love decided the time was right for Art, not when she decided it was. And besides, she had come to trust The Great Love, so there was no hurry; he always did what was best.

Eventually, at about one o'clock, they both yawned for the third time and decided it was time for sleep. They weren't much for overt expressions, but this time it came so naturally from them – they declared in very tender terms their love for each other and their joy at what the future might be like – and then they nestled down for sleep.

Art didn't dream…he snored. And Linda let him; she knew he needed his sleep for the work day ahead, and she could catch a nap after lunch if she needed it. Linda relaxed her senses until the snoring became nothing more than a purring sound in the distance, and then the River of Life closed in around her and she heard the Voice – he was singing. It was the most joyful song Linda had ever heard, and it was all about The Great Love and his enduring goodness. On and on the song went, rising to great crescendos of praise then subsiding into tender reflection of the love for humanity that flowed from his heart. Linda was caught up in the song; she couldn't help herself…such was the wonder of it. And she found that she knew the words too, and they burst out of her heart like a flood of thankfulness for The Great Love and his goodness and kindness.

The song rose up from deep inside Linda, but it was not audible; it was much lovelier than any human voice might produce – it was her heart singing, and it loved to sing. It seemed as though the prison of life had held her heart captive for an eternity, and it was making up for lost time now that it was free. Her heart recalled the songs of praise from an ancient time before the burdens of life had dimmed the songs from her memory, and they rose up from her innermost being with such passion that she could barely restrain herself from overflowing into tears.

Then she heard the others.

The rising and falling of other grateful hearts seeped into her, and she found herself praising The Great Love with thousands upon thousands of others, all reaching out to him as the overflow of their grateful hearts, because such a flood of praise cannot be held back by those who have been set free – it must burst forth, it must be released…just as they have been released.

There was movement – people running and dancing, hearts in motion with the sheer joy of being held by his extravagant love, spontaneously and uninhibitedly expressing the gift of divine life that was shared by the great assembly of the loved.

The awe of it was completely overwhelming…in part because the expression of praise that Linda was sharing in was more exhilarating than anything she had ever known in her life. But more than that, the more The Great Love was magnified in praise, the more his love for her was also magnified in her own heart. It seemed that the great throng of worshippers could not outgive The Great Love who was the object of their worship – and the more they expressed their joy, the more he expressed his love.

It was perfection, and even more than that…it was heaven.

Linda knew at last the point of it all; she understood that The Great Love created her (and all of humanity) out of the overflow of his extravagant love – with the single purpose that she would know him and his great heart for her, and out of that knowing she would make her home in that love.

Linda lay that way for a long time, revelling in the intensity of her new understanding and the sheer eminence and grandeur of it all. The River of Life flowed relentlessly with divine love – in fact, the River of Life was divine love – yet she had lived her whole life not realising what she was in. It was flowing all around her, but the more physically tangible reality of the natural realm had hid it all from her view.

And now The Great Love was showing her the truth. The tangible reality of the physical realm was losing its hold on her; it was being overtaken by the true purpose of her eternal design – that she would return to the original intent of her maker and allow his great love to hold her.

The prospect of living that way had never really occurred to Linda before; her life had always been held in place by the people and events that unfolded on a daily basis all around her – they seemed to have a way of containing her and determining her existence. But the thought that she could be contained by something other than her circum-stances had never even seemed like a possibility; it was beyond the realms of reason – yet she knew in her heart that it was her destiny, and she felt herself smile inside.

It was clear now from her conversations with Art, that all the self-imprisoning that life had conspired against them was just a small part of the picture. There was so much more to them than could be seen by the naked eye. They were the offspring of the greatest love in the universe, and beyond the universe even – all of eternity too – and she decided there and then to live that way.

Funny, she mused, *here I am a very average person living a very ordinary life, with a very normal family in a very plain house, yet I am the daughter of The Great Love – who would have thought?*

Linda couldn't switch off her brain; she had never lain awake all night, but it was looking like this might be another first. She drifted between conscious thought and the deep inner place beyond it, not quite knowing whether she was in one or the other, just aware that there was a re-education taking place in her – a kind of reconnection between the outer and the inner, and they were coming into agreement and becoming one.

Linda reflected on the day by the river when she had felt herself floating, leaving herself behind and looking down at things from a great height. She understood now that it was her inner self that was looking down on her outer self who was sitting in the deck chair far below. But now she also sensed that a wonderful reunion was taking place between her two selves; it was a rejoining of the Linda she had known all her life with the Linda that The Great Love knew. She felt that she was being reintroduced to a person she had heard about but not actually met, a foreign someone who was recorded in her ancient mythology, lost somewhere in distant folklore rather than present-day reality – and now here she was meeting herself for the first time and liking herself a lot.

And she could see what The Great Love saw, and why he loved her so much.

At six-thirty, Art began to stir and Linda watched him come awake. "Good morning," she greeted him brightly, "did you sleep well?"

"I did, though I could have used a few more hours," Art replied, "but you look especially fresh for someone who talked until one in the morning."

Linda gave him one of her big smiles, kissed him on the forehead and asked if he would like coffee. She bought two steaming cups back to bed, and they sipped and chatted casually until it was time for Art to get moving.

The family soon began the usual flurry of activity that marked the beginning of another busy day, and Linda heaved a big sigh of relief when the last one was on their way and she had the house to herself.

Strangely Linda didn't feel at all tired for having had no sleep; in fact, she felt quite invigorated. She had an errand today, one that gave her just a slight quiver of excitement, one that marked their new beginning. There was shopping to do, and she needed to wrap a present. Linda loved surprises.

CHAPTER 18

SURPRISED

The family drifted home one by one, with Art coming in last just after five o'clock – a lot earlier than the day before, and in a lot better mood. Dinner at the Linden house was livelier these days, chattering about the day's activities and the people involved had taken over from the more solemn meal times they had previously known. It had become the best part of the day that mixed good food with fun banter, and occasionally a more serious conversation…and they all loved it.

When dinner was over and before anyone could get up, Linda announced that she had something important to do. She produced from her secret spot in the pantry a beautifully wrapped present and handed it to Art and sweetly said, "For my wonderful husband and best friend, for no reason except that I love you." The rest all looked at each other with very mystified faces; this never happened in their family. Spontaneity never happened unless it was a birthday perhaps.

"Open it, Dad" urged Stevie and Kate at exactly the same time, and laughed because of it.

Art opened it with care, giving just the right amount of time to the task to show Linda that he was both surprised and touched. *A History of Poetry – from Wordsworth to*

Tennyson was the title that leapt off the cover as the wrapping fell open. Art was speechless, not quite knowing what to say, and yet knowing that this was more than a gift of kindness; it was his first step back into the life of his dreams.

"Thank you, my darling," was all he could say, because he knew that if he said more, there would be tears; and he didn't want the kids to wonder what was going on.

With the table cleaned and the dishes done, the family drifted off to do the things that suited them, leaving Art and Linda to a cup of tea in the kitchen. As the tea brewed, Art sat down with his book and turned the first page. A poem by Wordsworth presented itself, and Art recalled it from a lifetime ago. 'I Wandered Lonely as a Cloud' was the title, and he identified with the sentiment of it, but the words of the poem were full of promise and hope; and in that moment his love for literature was reawakened.

"This is the best thing you could have done for me, Linda. I feel like all the years since I last read the works of the great masters have been all swallowed up, and I am back in the high school library soaking up the pages again. Thank you so much; this means more than I can say."

Another big smile from Linda, and then she left the room to give Art some space to reacquaint himself with the lost years of his youth. He was swimming in a new river, a river filled with well-crafted words and deep meaning, a river that he thought had dried up; instead, that river had been miraculously flooded with water again to refresh his parched soul.

So many of the old poems spoke of rivers: 'The Lady of Shalott' by Lord Tennyson, 'To the River Charles' by Henry Wadsworth Longfellow, 'My River Runs to Thee' by Emily Dickinson, 'Looking Glass River' by Robert Louis Stephenson – so much so, that Art's thoughts began to drift that way. He wondered why the masters all seemed to be linked in some way…by the same river theme.

You're in the wrong river; it isn't what you think it is, played on his mind. This was more than simply rediscovering his love of literature; it was about rediscovering himself. It was about Art Linden the man, not just Art Linden who might have been a teacher.

Art admitted to himself that there were some things he could do and some things he could not, and rediscovering the real Art Lindon fell into the latter category. He wished he was more like Stevie and could disconnect himself from the real world by the simple act of lapsing into daydreaming, but he was too practical for that and far too grown up. Life had dulled the spontaneous sense of wonder and anticipation that was once within him, and he quietly hoped that the pages before him might reignite the embers that dimly glowed in his heart.

"How's it going, Art?" asked Linda, peeping around the kitchen door. "You ready for a cup of tea?" As much as Art was enjoying the reading, he was ready to talk some more – he was ready to continue the unpacking process that had started the night before. He had a taste for talking about himself in a way that had previously seemed shallow or self-indulgent, and now he wanted to get whatever it was that was hidden away inside him out in the open where he could have a good look at it and decide what needed to be done.

"Linda, I know you want me to have my dream back, but I'm not sure it fits me now as much as it might have when I was eighteen. But I think I want to get myself back – I think this is about more than just a missed career; it is about rediscovering who I really am. I don't want so much to reclaim the lost years, but I do want to reconnect myself with the guy I used to be before my father's sense of obligation moulded me into his stoic image."

Linda took a deep breath; she hoped this was the right moment to let Art in on her new life. But she knew she had to tread carefully so that his tendency towards retreating into rational thinking didn't obstruct the flow of realisation that was beginning to invade the workings of his mind.

"You remember a few weeks ago when I grounded Stevie?" she asked. "That was because he tried to explain his disappearance by presenting me with an explanation that seemed so far-fetched that I accused him of telling ridiculous made-up stories instead of telling the truth."

"I remember you were pretty steamed up about it" recalled Art, "but what has that got to do with discovering who I really am?"

"And do you remember that I cancelled Stevie's grounding after just a few days when it was supposed to go for a month? I did that because he was telling the truth, and I had to concede that I was wrong.

"And do you remember when we went to the river for a picnic and I told you that I hadn't seen the river even though I had been there just the day before…because I didn't open my eyes? Well, this is connected to all those things that seemed so weird to you, so I'm going to need you to be very patient with me as I talk you through it."

"I know that there has been something different going on," admitted Art, "and the other night when you shone with such inner beauty, I had to admit to myself that it was pretty special. So I will do my best to hear your story, Linda, but you will also need to be patient with me if I don't get it."

"Okay, it's a deal; we will be very patient with each other," she agreed.

Linda had no reluctance or embarrassment; this was not a matter that caused her any hesitation at all, because this conversation was about her true self now. It had gone way beyond her earlier hopes and dreams and had become her deepest reality. But she shared her story tentatively for Art's sake, because she knew from experience that he had yet to let go, and so a lot of reflection was still ahead for him. She told him about the Voice that spoke to her from her deepest self, and she told him about the Life, and the river within the river that flowed from the source of all love; and she told him about The Great Love himself, and how she had made her home in his infinite love for her.

Art sat passively taking it all in, honouring Linda in his silence, yet wrestling with the strange and impossible notion that all she said might be true.

"I will need some time," confessed Art. "This flies in the face of all that is reasonable and provable; I can't just embrace this on face value, and in fact I'm having diffi-culty even believing it…except for the change I see in you. It will take me some time to digest, and then even longer to act…if I am able to."

Linda responded with the same words that the Voice had said to her, "You are right; it cannot begin for you yet because you have yet to let go, and you need some time of reflection for that to happen."

There was no coercion here. Linda knew that she was not a part of the journey that Art must make, and that she had to let him go there alone. Yet she trusted implicitly that the Voice, and the River of Life, and The Great Love would bring Art through. So she rested in the assurance that Art would let go in his own time – and if it took a little longer, then that was alright with her, because she knew that he could embrace the realm of the River of Life only if he had also come to terms with relinquishing the hold that the natural realm had over him.

In spite of Linda's patience and confidence that everything would come to pass for Art just as it had for her, she asked The Great Love to help Art. She knew in her heart even before she asked that she was asking for the same thing that was already burning in The Great Love's own heart, and that he loved Art as much as she did, and just as much as he loved her too.

So she released Art to the care of The Great Love. As far as she was concerned, Art was no longer her responsibility; he had departed on his own journey, and all she could do was exercise the patience that she promised.

"Goodnight, Art," whispered Linda.

"Thanks for the book, Honey. I'll be okay," replied Art.

CHAPTER 19

PATIENCE

The days slowly turned into a week, and Art and Linda had not spoken of it again. There was a civilized tension in the air, but they didn't discuss it; they just acted as normal as possible…and Linda waited.

Under the surface, Art was stewing in it. As much as he wanted to retreat to the relative safety of the higher ground of his logical thoughts, he found himself continually pulled back into a mystery which could not be so easily explained – and it threatened to dismantle the walls he had built around himself to keep control of his life.

Art read his book from cover to cover; he read every poem until they began to be etched in his mind, and then he read them all again and again until he thought he knew every word by heart. He came upon the poem by Robert Wadsworth Lowry for the third, fourth or maybe fifth time, only this time he read it more slowly because it seemed to be calling to him:

> *Shall we gather at the river*
>
> *Where bright angel feet have trod;*
>
> *With its crystal tide forever*
>
> *Flowing by the throne of God?*

'Shall we gather at the river…flowing by the throne of God?' It felt like an invitation to him to attend a meeting of hearts, and for some inexplicable reason, he wanted to go…in fact, he felt strangely compelled to go.

"Honey, I'm going for a walk; I'll be down at the river." Art got up and wandered down to the river mindlessly, as if carried along by another who knew what was happening and had guaranteed Art's attendance. He almost stumbled along, not unwillingly but not intentionally either; he was conveyed there by the power of an eternal appointment which was made by another and of which he understood very little.

He walked along the water's edge and, after a little while, noticed a fish in the shallows. The fish was in water not deep enough to swim out of; it was stuck there, exhausted and slowly dying, incapable of helping itself.

As Art looked at the fish and the unfolding demise occurring before his eyes, he heard the words again, "You're in the wrong river." And as he pondered those words and looked at the fish, it spoke to him in an exhausted squeaky kind of way: "Help, I'm stuck. You don't know me, but I'm Eric, a friend of Stevie's. Can you please pick me up and put me back in the river?"

To say that Art was shocked would be an understatement; maybe this was why he felt compelled to come down to the river – to save a fish in trouble. So Art pulled himself together and kicked off his shoes and socks, then stepped into the shallows and bent down to gently gather up the fish before wading out into the deeper water and releasing it into safety.

The fish didn't move for a while; at first, it just floated there on its side, but slowly its strength seemed to return and it began to flex its tail and fins – but it didn't swim away. "Sit down," the fish ordered Art. "We need to talk, and I can't do that in the shallows; you'll have to sit where you are and get wet."

Taking orders from a recently rescued fish was so surprisingly out of left field for Art that he complied against his better judgement and sat down in the water until it came up to his middle. Eric was swimming freely by now and circled Art a few times before speaking. "Firstly, thank you for rescuing me; I really needed your help. I was completely stuck and had no way to save myself, and now I would like to help you because you are stuck too and need rescuing in your own way."

"The only problem is," confessed Eric, "I'm new at this too. I've been swimming around in the Hopkins River all my life, just letting life happen to me and living by my wits. My friend Leo knows all about this stuff…but I didn't believe him. I thought he was just rambling on about some silly ideas he had in his head that I didn't think I needed to know about – and I told him so. But today when I got stuck, I realised that Leo has been right all along. There is more going on than I can see – and I need to get with the program and be a smart fish.

"So what are we going to do, Art?" asked Eric, "I'm glad you helped me, but I'm still in the Hopkins River – I could get stuck again anytime. I'm just that kind of fish."

Talking to fish didn't come easily to Art, but the conversation seemed to be going somewhere so he overcame his reluctance and tentatively launched in. "Well, I don't know Eric, there seems to be something we are both missing – I can almost touch it, but it's just beyond my reach…like talking to you. It doesn't make sense – but here I am doing it anyway."

"You're kidding yourself," said a rather large cod that had popped his head through the surface.

"You must be Leo," stated Art.

"Yep, you got that right. I'm Leo and pleased to meet any friend of Stevie's, but that's about the only thing you have right. You aren't going to get a handle on any of this until you admit to yourself that there is more going on than you can see."

After Art got over his surprise to be in conversation with a second fish, he tentatively gave Leo permission to go on and assured him he was listening.

"For starters, you both know that you're in the wrong river, don't you?" Art nodded and Eric wriggled his top fin, which was like a nod for cod fish. "And you are both finally beginning to realise that you can't do much to help yourselves – sure, you can do each other favours in the Hopkins River, but you can't find your way into the invisible river within the river by yourselves." Again, they nodded and twitched.

"The river within the river is wide open to you both, and it is actually flowing all around you both – but it cannot give you the Life you both need while you are also drawing your life from the visible one. Visible things are not meant to do that, so you must choose which river will provide for you; and you are presently choosing the natural river to do that. You can work hard to make a living, Art, or feed yourself on the food that floats by in the river, Eric; but that is not what I am talking about. I am talking about the life source of your deepest self, not merely your physical well-being – do you understand?"

This time there were no nods, and Eric's fin didn't even flutter. "Well, give it time," said Leo, and with that he winked and was off. Cod fish don't have eyelids, so that wink was unexpected and a little bit weird, but it was that kind of day, so Art didn't dwell on it.

After exchanging a few more pleasantries, Eric said he needed to be on his way and, with a flip of his tale, was gone – leaving Art sitting in the river up to his middle.

Art didn't see any reason to move; the water was warm, and the river seemed to enliven his thoughts, so he stayed where he was for a bit longer. It seemed to Art that Leo was suggesting that there was another unseen river which flowed inside the Hopkins River and perhaps everywhere else too, which certainly lined up with the conversation he had with Linda. Maybe he was in that unseen river right now and just didn't realise it; maybe he couldn't see it because he didn't believe it was there.

"Art, what are you doing sitting in the water?" Linda had come down to the river because he had been gone for so long.

"Long story," said Art, as Linda kicked off her shoes and waded over to him.

Art began to stand up, but Linda put her hand on his shoulder and said, "Stay there; it looks a bit quirky seeing you sitting in the river fully dressed, but it kind of appeals to me so I'm going to join you." And with that, she sat down next to him with a plop, rested her head on his shoulder and waited for the long story.

"This has been the weirdest day, Linda; I've been talking to fish." Yet Linda could see that Art was troubled by more than that; he had an internal wrestling going on that was affecting him deeply.

"You mean Eric and Leo" asked Linda. "Stevie told me about them. He said that Eric was a bit dim and didn't know how to get out of a wet paper bag, and Leo was a bit gruff on the outside but a pretty smart fish when you got to know him."

"That's about it," agreed Art sadly, "that pretty much describes what just happened here."

"I'm afraid I may be a bit of an Eric," admitted Art, choking up, "I don't know how to get out of a wet paper bag – I'm stuck, Linda, and I don't know what to do." Once Art had let the words come out of his mouth, the tears came too, great sobbing tears of anguish began to wrack him, and a lifetime of restraint finally was given release as he cried like a little boy…a little boy who was sitting up to his middle in the river with his wife gently comforting him…and each tear seemed to be caught by someone who understood him and cared deeply, but as yet could not be seen by him.

"I've tried so hard to be strong," he said, "I've tried to keep going and carry the burdens of the past as well as toughening up for the burdens that lay in the future; but I'm spent. My resolve is all gone, and my dad isn't here to tell me what to do next."

"You know, Art, your dad didn't know what to do next either. He lived his whole life fighting to keep his head above water too…all he did was survive; he wasn't actually living. He spent his whole life fighting for survival in the natural realm, when he was meant to rest in the goodness of the River of Life."

"But if Dad didn't know what to do, who does?" questioned Art gloomily.

"It's time for you to ask The Great Love that question, Art. He is the father you can speak to about this, the one who will lead you into the River of Life. But we should get up and go home; it's getting a bit cold, and besides, someone might wander by and see us like this and think we're crazy."

CHAPTER 20

ON BEING CRAZY

The battle was between his ears; Art knew that – he was wrestling with logic, and logic told him he was crazy to entertain ideas about living in another realm. Nobody relocated their existence into an unseen realm; it just wasn't possible – in fact, it was downright ridiculous.

Backwards and forwards the battle raged in his head until Linda suggested something right out of the blue. "Stop thinking with your head, and start thinking with your heart – go against your logical processes and give The Great Love permission to show you what you cannot see."

Art was rapidly running out of options. He knew all about prayer from church – which was more of a ritual than an actual person-to-person conversation – but Linda seemed to be suggesting that he go even further than that and engage the very core of his existence with this unseen being, not just his spoken words. And she seemed to have this unseen person in a completely different frame than he was used to. She didn't call him God – she called him The Great Love. Could they be the same person?

"Is God The Great Love?" asked Art.

"I don't know," said Linda. "At least he's not the God I grew up with; there doesn't seem to be much common ground between them in my mind. I just don't feel comfortable calling The Great Love 'God'. It throws me off somehow – I don't know him as God because God means something different to me than what I have come to know in The Great Love."

"How so?" asked Art.

"Well, The Great Love gives love – I don't need to qualify for it by being good or doing anything really. I just need to give him permission to have my life," she explained. "My relationship with The Great Love is more about him than it is about me; I just allow him to love me, and it flows from there. But my idea of God is not like that. He seems to have expectations of me that I have to meet; he seems to want me to fix up my life to receive his favour – it's like a continual process of self-maintenance."

"But The Great Love came to me in my brokenness, not in my togetherness – and I love him for that. So I guess the answer is no, I don't think they are the same" said Linda thoughtfully.

That response helped Art because he also knew that he had nothing to bring to the table. It helped him to think that fixing things was not his job; his only part was to give permission. He wasn't really sure what that looked like in real time because he didn't know The Great Love yet to give him that permission – but he quietly asked The Great Love to show himself, so that he could move forward.

Art had been stuck just like Eric, and he decided that he wasn't able to clear the log-jam caused by his conflicting thoughts; so he simply stepped around it and acted upon his uncertainty instead of his certainty. Art had spent a lifetime acting upon his certainty; work equals pay, self-effort equals self-respect, that sort of thing – but now he decided that the waiting game was over. This was never going to make sense to his rational mind; that kind of logical thinking was just too ingrained in him – so he looked to his uncertainty instead.

If Art was going to become not stuck, then he acknowledged that it wouldn't come from his own self-effort or reasoning.

Having asked The Great Love to show himself, Art let the whole matter go; it was out of his hands now – he could no sooner get The Great Love to show up than fly to the moon. He didn't even have any personal experience with The Great Love to hang his confidence on… except maybe talking fish, and a wife who radiated new beauty, and poetry that spoke to him.

More days passed and Art was about ready to let the whole thing drop. He was sitting on the porch enjoying a quiet moment with the newspaper when he heard the faintest voice. He looked all around him to see who it was, but there was no-one; so he wrote it off as people walking down by the river.

"Art." He heard it again, coming from such a distance that it was barely audible.

"Who is it?" asked Art. "And where are you?"

"Art."

There it was again, so distant – yet there all the same. This time Art whispered with trepidation "I'm listening."

The Voice had to speak through Art's many layers of built-up resistance; there was so much of the natural realm to penetrate with Art because he had dug himself in so deeply over his many years of self-dependence. But Art had opened the door, and the Voice was determined to walk through it in spite of Art's ingrained resistance.

Art sat absolutely still; not a muscle twitched, not even a thought passed through his mind – he was ready to hear.

"Art, I need you to do something for me," said the Voice, but Art couldn't imagine what – he had already acknowledged his hopelessness. "Art, I want you to allow me to speak to you from your book of poetry. Until you have learned to trust your heart, I would like your permission to explain to you the truth you seek by a means that is easier for you – I need to bypass your dependence on logic."

In quite stammering speech, Art gave the Voice his permission, and then he felt a warmth fill him that had never filled him before, and his anticipation rose with it. Art didn't really know how this was supposed to work, so he picked up the book. After looking at it on his lap for several minutes, he decided to just lift the cover and read from the page that fell open. It was not a very scientific approach, but then this whole thing was beyond his ingrained systematic approach to life – so he just decided to do it that way. The first poem to present itself was the classic by Robert Frost 'The Road not Taken', and it was not until the last verse that the words leapt off the page and into Art's heart:

I shall be telling this with a sigh

Somewhere ages and ages hence:

Two roads diverged in a wood, and I—

I took the one less traveled by,

And that has made all the difference.

I took the road less travelled, and that has made all the difference. Art repeated these words to himself over and over again. And then he reflected on the words that had been etched into his mind these past weeks. "You are in the wrong river," he whispered to himself. And then he spoke to the Voice…if he was listening, "I think I am trying to make my life different while remaining on the wrong road. I don't think the road I am on allows for the difference I want…I think it always produces the same imprisoned results. The road I am on can only produce sameness; to have difference I need to take a different road…"

You're in the wrong river.

And the warmth flooded through him again, filling him with the assurance that the message from the Voice had been heard – and Art sat there revelling in the warmth and the truth that was unfolding to him. There was another path, it was less travelled and unfamiliar; the different life he sought could not be found on the path he had spent his life walking on – to have life, he must change paths. It was not a matter of improving his management of life on the path he was presently on; he had to leave that path for a completely different and unfamiliar path.

That was enough for one day. It was enough to have received one message from the Voice; he knew that 'letting go' was not a hurried process, and he needed to allow this truth to be established in him for the next one to be laid over it.

Art wanted to be sure that he was completely convinced that he really was in the wrong river (or on the wrong path) before opening the book again. If it took a day, or a week, or a month, he wouldn't go looking for the next truth until this one was actually true for him.

THE TRUTH

The following days were something of a wrestling match for Art. Sometimes the natural realm would assert itself and convince Art that in this life there was no other realm, and at other times the river within the river seemed to flow as plain as day before his very eyes.

It was during a time when the natural realm was very insistent that the penny dropped. *The natural realm is right in what it is saying 'in this life there is no other realm' – the only way I can live in the River of Life is to die to the realm that is presently holding me,* he thought. Art knew that this was not a physical death; clearly Linda was still alive and kicking, and perhaps even more so since going through her own death – but still, there it was. He was beginning to think he must die in some way.

Dying is not a thing to which the living are immediately drawn; we don't by nature relish the idea or embrace the journey. Yet, if we knew what lay beyond death, we would let go of the hold that this life has over us in a heartbeat. Art didn't really know what lay beyond the natural realm; he didn't know all that much about the River of Life at all, but he was willing to know, and that was the main thing.

As was becoming his habit, he whispered to himself (and the Voice if he was listening), that he was willing to change rivers if he could just glimpse the alternative.

The book fell open once again and by chance to the poem by Rumi. 'Defeated by Love' looked up at him, and the whole of the poem spoke this time.

> *—The sky was lit*
>
> *by the splendour of the moon,*
>
> *So powerful*
>
> *I fell to the ground.*
>
> *Your love*
>
> *has made me sure,*
>
> *I am ready to forsake*
>
> *this worldly life*
>
> *and surrender*
>
> *to the magnificence*
>
> *of your Being.*

Words can speak when we are ready for them to…and Art was ready.

He pondered the possibility: could a love so magnificent really exist that we might allow ourselves to be defeated by it and surrender to it? If it were possible, then it would be the only reason why someone might willingly die and forsake this worldly life. But it seemed too extravagant; too opposed to the way he perceived life and its cause-and-effect rules. To forsake this worldly life and surrender to a love so magnificent was more than he could ever dream of, more than he had ever permitted himself to hope for.

Art's thoughts had become poetic in themselves as the splendour of it all began to fill his imagination – and the warmth returned once again and rushed through his being with the urgency of love that must find its beloved and be at home there.

Linda had been out for a walk and saw as she reached the front gate Art slumped in his chair on the verandah with his book open in his lap. *He's asleep,* she thought – at least, his eyes were closed – so she tiptoed to get past without disturbing him.

The nearer she got to Art, the more she felt the presence of The Great Love; there was a deep warmth all around him, luxuriating and tender, yet intense and determined. She felt herself drawn in to it. The radiance was like a magnet which called deeply to her to come and be satu-rated in love, and because she had long ago let go of her old life, she responded easily to the call and let the love fill her and consume her all over again.

To remain standing was impossible, so Linda lay down on the grass in their little front yard just in front of the verandah and absorbed wave after wave, allowing the love to wash over and through her, cleaning and purifying to the most unsearchably deep part of her heart, until all that was left of her was pure love.

Linda was exhausted from the experience. Art was affected in his own way too – because now he was assured that the River of Life was worth dying for. He knew deep inside that the life waiting for him in The Great Love was beyond his imagination and that it was his destiny to go there. Yet only one realm could truly hold him – the seen or the unseen. The source of his life must be anchored – but even more than that, actually lived out – in one or the other.

He opened his eyes, slowly adjusting his sight to the bright daylight, and saw Linda on the grass. Thinking she was sleeping – just as she had thought he was sleeping – he watched her there, strangely though not really thinking that it was odd that his wife was lying on the grass in front of him. And as he watched, he saw that her lips were moving, just barely but moving all the same; no audible sound escaped her so she wasn't trying to speak something out – instead she seemed to be taking something in, something wonderful and deeply joyful was happening to Linda. Art watched it happening and marvelled at the spectacle of it.

Art observed first hand a phenomenon that few in this world ever see: a human being visible before his eyes receiving love from another realm that was not visible to him. And it helped him understand something that eludes most people: true love is not expressed by giving things – like material blessings and favourable circumstances; it is expressed by giving itself. As he watched, he realised that Linda was absorbing the nature of The Great Love; she was becoming a vessel of love herself.

Art had thought that love began with a decision to love and was then expressed by a physical act of kindness or charity, but this was much more than that. This love was filling Linda for no purpose other than that it must, straight out of the source and into the object of that love – because The Great Love must love, or else his true self is merely constrained and measured just like a man.

Eventually it subsided, and Linda opened her eyes. Seeing Art was still there, she chuckled at him because he was staring at her again like the time he said she had become beautiful. "What?" she asked.

"That's what I want to know – what just happened?" he probed.

"Well, Art, I got caught up in the warmth that was radiating from you as you were slumped in the chair, and I just let The Great Love pour his love into me too – it was like I was drinking pure love directly from the divine source of it."

"Okay, you are right; I did feel an overwhelming and urgent warmth rush through me, but you seemed to go to a whole other level – you seemed to dissolve into it. I've never seen anything like it."

"You will, Art, just wait and see. Now that you have started, there is no stopping; prepare yourself to be dismantled and then reborn into your true self – the one that receives love easily, just as The Great Love first planned you would when he conceived you in his heart in eternity." And she smiled that smile.

Kate and her friend Bethany came walking down the street talking and laughing. They said goodbye at the gate to Kate's house, and Bethany kept on her way home while Kate pushed open the gate. She was caught by surprise to see her mum and dad sitting on the grass talking; that never happened in her family.

"Hi, Mum and Dad, what are you doing there?" she asked with a weird look on her face.

"It's a long story, Kate," replied Linda, "but watch this space. Your family is doing a lot of new things lately, and sitting on the grass talking is not the least of them."

Kate rolled her eyes and kept walking; little did she know what lay ahead. Linda followed her into the house to begin dinner and left Art stretched out on the grass pondering the events of the day. There was so much to reflect upon, so much to absorb and understand…yet so much that simply could not be understood. It was beyond reason, so Art simply allowed it to settle in him – he just decided to let it be what it was, the most extraordinary day of his life…so far.

"What's next?" he whispered cautiously.

CHAPTER 21
THE DYING

The next day was Saturday, and the family had disappeared in one direction or another while Art sat in the easy chair by the window with the book in his lap. He knew today was very important – perhaps the most important day of his life – because he knew that today was the day when he would die.

There was no fear, just anticipation of making the crossing.

Not that he knew what to do next, but he knew that the Voice knew, and that meant that he would know in good time.

He handled the book with tenderness. It was the best gift he had ever been given, and soon it would conduct him on his final journey out of this world and into the River of Life forever. Yet he was reluctant to begin; he loved his life in this world, and one part of him didn't want to lose his attachment to it, while the other part of him was straining to leave.

Then the Voice spoke. "You are not leaving this world, Art; you are dying to it as the source of your being. In its place, the life that flows from The Great Love will be your source. No longer will you look to your self-effort or good living to give you life; now you will receive it directly from the River of Life. The world that you love will still be there to enjoy, but its hold on you will be gone."

Art nodded. He understood. He was ready.

As he began to open the book, his arm bumped his cup of coffee. It began to slip off the arm of the chair, and in recovering it, he tore the page in front of him from side to side. He was so disappointed and about to get up and find the sticky tape to repair it as best he could when he glanced down and noticed two pages had overlapped, and two poems had become linked as one. The last stanza of a poem by the great man John Keats, 'A Thing of Beauty', was lying over a poem by Henry Van Dyke, 'For Katrina's Sun Dial'…and they read as one.

> *And such too is the grandeur of the dooms*
>
> *We have imagined for the mighty dead;*
>
> *An endless fountain of immortal drink,*
>
> *Pouring unto us from the heaven's brink.*
>
> *Time is too slow for those who wait,*
>
> *Too swift for those who fear,*
>
> *Too long for those who grieve,*
>
> *Too short for those who rejoice,*
>
> *But for those who love,*
>
> *time is Eternity.*

For some, the significance of these two poems read together might be lost; but for Art, the poignancy was altogether beyond belief and way beyond coincidence. He pictured an endless fountain of immortal life continually pouring over the brink of heaven and into his innermost being. It was divine love flowing from eternity and into time because the two realms had become one for him; he would be sustained by the life of heaven while living on the earth – for him, time would be swallowed up in eternity.

And as the warmth rose up and filled him, beginning at his toes and inhabiting every crevice of his being to the very top of his head, he whispered the words that only eternity can comprehend: "Today I die that I might live anew in the River of Life."

In that instant, Arthur Linden ceased to exist – he was gone.

For anyone looking on in the natural realm, that may have seemed like a nonsense; Art was still there, still breathing, his heart still pumping blood through his veins – but on the other side an entirely new man was born… not a flesh-and-blood man, but a new kind of man from a realm where flesh and blood did not contribute to one's identity, because that was provided by something far greater and far more capable of holding a man in place – the life that flows from the heart of The Great Love.

Art had come home to eternity, and eternity was very glad to have him.

He knew in his heart that he was still himself; the old Art remained…yet he was so deeply transformed that he barely resembled his old inner self. He had been made so new and clean on the inside that it was as if he had been born a second time as the same person, a person who was fashioned from the heart of The Great Love himself.

Art knew this; he had been well prepared by all that had taken place in the weeks leading up to this moment, and the import of what had just taken place was not lost on him. The warmth that filled him was all the evidence he needed, and the rest of it, whatever it might be, lay ahead. It was not a matter of hoping things would be different; that didn't even enter Art's head. As far as he was concerned, his old life was gone, dead, never to be revived again – and he had no future but the River of Life.

The decision to die that Art had made was final – such was the gravity of it to him – and from this moment on he would wait for the River of Life to direct things. If nothing happened, it made no difference to Art, because his decision was not about getting things to happen. It was about living from another source of life.

He had been converted in the true sense of the word; he could no longer be sustained by this world even if he wanted to – he was no longer that kind of being. He had been converted back into his original design and all that it contained, and the ways of the world were now strangely foreign – all that lay ahead for him now was eternity in the River of Life.

And he had not the slightest doubt that The Great Love would carry him and hold him – that was just how eternity worked.

He looked down at his book again to read the poems over, but he couldn't find the torn page; everything was intact again, and the two poems were separated once again on their original pages. He knew then that from that point on, the Voice would speak to him directly without the addition of any physical device.

It would be heart to heart and Spirit to spirit.

CHAPTER 22

KATE

"Dad, you seem to sit around so much these days; it's all you seem to do?" commented Kate, noticing that he was still sitting in the easy chair by the window just as he had been that morning.

"Hi, Kate, you are very observant; I've been completely engrossed in the new book your mum gave me," replied Art, giving Kate the space to take this further or not.

Kate was not infected by the timidity of her parents or the insular characteristics of her brother; she was completely 'out there' in her speech and appearance. Always moving, always pushing some invisible boundary with her wild hair like an early warning device that announced her arrival. Linda and Art had long ago given up trying to affect her appearance; she would dress how she liked, and the darker the better.

"Hmm, that sounds like a lame deflection, Dad," returned Kate. "Gotta go!" And she was out the door.

It was clear to Art that Kate had picked up that something new was going on in her family, and just as clear that she didn't want to know about it and have it cramp her style. *Fifteen-year-old black sheep are even harder to transform than the rest of us,* he thought, *and Kate's hostility towards acknowledging or even admitting this new thing exists is increasing by the day.*

"Was that Kate I heard flying out of the house like a whirlwind? She never sits still for a minute anymore," frowned Linda.

"Come and sit with me, Honey. This is all so new to me that it helps me to talk it through a bit more."

"Okay, but just for a little while. I promised Stevie I would take a snack to him down at the river."

"Well, why don't I wander along, and we can talk while we walk; let me know when you're ready to go."

As they walked and talked about all that had recently taken place in their lives, it became apparent that they had never before been more on the same page. They were finishing each other's sentences and laughing spontaneously and warmly at the joy of it all.

They were coming down over the last rise and wandering over to where they could see Stevie in the distance where the river bends back on itself when Linda said, "What do you think Kate makes of everything, Art? She seems to be almost antagonistic – like she's running away from us?"

"It's what I wanted to talk to you about, Linda; she seems to be distancing herself from us. It's like she is trying too hard to be someone else, but she's not sure who." They talked it back and forward as they were coming up to Stevie and finally decided that they could entrust Kate into the care of The Great Love – one way or another she would 'let go' and embrace him. No other option seemed possible in spite of the tension that was in the air.

"Hey, Mum, hey, Dad," greeted Stevie, "the fish are a bit slow today – but it sure is cool being here all the same."

Then Stevie followed up with a comment they didn't expect from a ten-year-old. "Mum, Dad, I think Kate needs to find The Great Love – it shouldn't be just us three; it doesn't seem right that we all have such an amazing new life and Kate is living back in the old… isn't there something we can do?"

"You're right, Stevie," Linda agreed, "but we need to give her space and entrust her into The Great Love's care – don't you think?" They all agreed that Kate would get there in her own time, and there was little they could do to hurry things along, because it wasn't about making a few minor adjustments, it was about choosing to die… and that could not be rushed.

"Don't be home late, Stevie. It's getting dark early now."

As they walked back home, Linda and Art reflected on their own journey out of the realm of nature and into the River of Life. They had both arrived in completely different ways and had to overcome completely different personal obstacles. Yet Stevie had simply stepped right in; he had no reluctance because he came as a little child, and his ability to dream and imagine new things had made his journey so effortless. He simply responded to his heart.

Whether Kate would do the same remained to be seen, but both Linda and Art had some doubts; she was so doggedly headstrong and impulsive – she would do it her way. Added to that, she seemed to be nursing a resentment that was new, as if she knew deep down that her family was changing, and she was digging herself in against that change.

Sunday morning arrived with the slow pace the family had established over many years. There was no rush; church wasn't until ten thirty, so a slow start was completely in order.

It wasn't until ten o'clock that Linda noticed Kate hadn't shown her face, so she went to her room to see what was holding her up. Kate was always on the move, and this was out of character.

"I'm not going to church, Mum," she almost spat out, "and you can't make me."

"But, Kate, we always go to church; we have your whole life. Now, come on; get dressed and I will make you a piece of toast to eat on the way." Linda fully expected Kate to drift out behind her, but nothing happened; Kate was holding her ground.

This was new territory for Linda, and Kate had all the fifteen-year-old tenacity needed to stand firm.

"Why don't you want to go, Kate?" Linda asked with concern.

"I just don't. I'm not going to church anymore…ever." It was so final that it took Linda quite by surprise. This was more than Kate being stubborn or headstrong; something had happened, and whatever it was fed on Kate's hostility and drew a new line between them.

"What is it, Kate, what's wrong?" But Kate clammed up; Linda would get no more out of her for now – the subject was closed until Kate reopened it. So Linda countered with her own deviation from the predictable:

"Well, Kate, if you're not going to church, then neither am I – we are a family, and that's more important to me than anything. I don't know what's troubling you Kate, but when you're ready to talk, I will be ready to listen… now, what do you want on your toast?"

Kate was no closer to talking when Linda brought the toast into her room, so she touched her lightly and brushed her hair off her face, and left her to herself. This was not like Kate; even at her most rebellious, she would always blurt out whatever was on her mind. She was a talker, not a clammer; and as Linda walked back to the kitchen, she quietly asked The Great Love what it was that was troubling Kate.

In the meantime, they agreed that Art and Stevie should go to church as Stevie was a monitor at Sunday school that week, and Linda would stay home with Kate.

Art found himself listening to the sermon but not hearing it; he was completely distracted by the trouble at home when he heard Pastor Meade say something that jerked his attention back to the present: "How can God answer your prayers and bless you if you don't live a life that pleases him?"

For the next fifteen minutes, Art thought about that; he thought about the cause-and-effect mindset which had underpinned his whole life, and in particular his Christian belief system – it was the foundational premise which seemed to be behind it all. He thought about the messages he heard most Sundays, which primarily related to morality, being good and a wide range of self-improvement programs – all motivated by the fact that Jesus had died for our sins, and therefore this was expected from us in return. And he wondered if there was something wrong with it all. It sounded right, but it unsettled him at the same time.

Not that he wasn't pleased to be saved by Jesus, but why did it all come down to being good so God would be happy? Surely God was happy because of something more reliable than human behaviour – it all seemed a little bit strange to Art for the first time in his life. He had never thought this way before, but now that he was, it was so blatantly obvious.

Art was not normally a man given to swimming against the stream; he was slow to express his opinion, particularly when it wasn't in line with the view of the majority – but in this instance, he was struggling to retain his composure. Art barely made it out of church without voicing his concerns out loud: *Why are we all so comfortable with a God who can never be completely happy with us?*

Art had been a churchgoer his whole life. All through his childhood and right up to the present day, he had never missed church unless he was sick or away from home; but this Sunday, he wished he had stayed home with Linda and Kate – such was the inner struggle that raged in him.

It wasn't until I met The Great Love that I became dissatisfied with God, he mused, *and now that I've met The Great Love I don't know what to do with God.* God had been safely contained in the pages of the Bible and in church on Sundays, but The Great Love changed all that with his inner presence which continually resonated so strongly in Art's heart…not just on Sundays, but for every moment of the day.

In short – Art liked The Great Love a lot more than he liked God.

But it wasn't quite as easy as that because Art had been a Christian his whole life; it was a part of him, and he couldn't just shrug it off. So Art reasoned that a tension existed – he knew God with his head, and he knew The Great Love with his heart. Art also knew that The Great Love understood this dilemma and would help him through it.

Art asked Linda how Kate was doing as he walked into the kitchen door.

"She just isn't herself, Art. Something is wrong, and she's shut down and won't talk about it."

"I'll make a cup of tea and take it to her room and see how she is myself."

A few minutes later, Art set Kate's cup down on the bedside table and settled down in her desk chair sipping his own cup. "Mum said you still haven't talked about what's bothering you about church. Well, Kate, I went to church this morning with Stevie, and the message from Pastor Meade got me so worked up, I almost stomped out of the place."

"Oh?" Kate tried to appear disinterested as she questioned in a deliberately casual tone, "Why?" She was still limiting her conversation to small bites, but enquiring with her eyes.

"Something is wrong with the message, Kate, and I can't quite put my finger on it – I just don't think I like God anymore."

"Huh. Well, I don't like God or the people you think you can respect but who lie to you," grunted Kate, arms crossed.

"Oh, okay. Tell me about that, Kate; tell me what has happened," her dad asked gently.

Kate didn't want to share; she hadn't planned to because she was feeling so mad and hemmed in. But a small crack appeared in the wall of her rigid determination, and against Kate's better judgement, it seemed to open up all on its own so that her self-protection couldn't stand against it. And gradually, with a weak voice and stammering lips, she told Art everything that had happened. The tears flowed as Kate explained her problem to Art, and he comforted her as only a dad can.

Kate explained how Dylan Meade had been appointed to lead the youth group and was in charge of everything now. The problem for Kate and some of the other girls was that while Dylan appeared to be a nice boy when he was in the public eye, he was lewd and sexually suggestive behind closed doors. Kate said that she had told him she didn't like it, but he said she should grow up and that his innuendos about sex were just the modern way of communicating – if she wanted to fit in, she should get with the program and start to be a part of the fun.

Kate felt tense and uncomfortable and wasn't prepared to do that, and now Dylan had singled her out as the butt of all his suggestive talk, even to the point of making up fantasies about Kate and spreading rumours about how she wanted to lose her virginity very soon to anyone who was willing.

Kate was a fun girl, but this was beyond fun, and all her teenage hormones raged at the indignation of it – she liked being the black sheep, but this was a step too far… even for her.

Kate sobbed as she leaned into her dad's strong arms, and as Art comforted her, he fumed inside with indignation that his little girl who had grown into an unruly teenager could be treated so badly.

"But isn't Dylan Pastor Meade's boy?" asked Art.

"Yes, he is, and that's why this is so hard," she sobbed. "We all thought he was nice until he showed his true colours, but now I can't go to church or youth group because he will say those things – I just can't be there anymore, ever."

"Don't worry, sweetheart. This will end today," Art promised.

"You don't understand, Dad, he will deny it. He'll say that I just made it up – he said he would if I ever told anyone. He said he will make up stories about me and spread lies about me being loose."

"One way or the other, this will end today," declared Art a second time. "Trust me, Kate, this will be exposed for what it is – it may take a little while, but the truth will be plainly seen and you will be released from all this foolishness."

Once again she received a loving kiss on the forehead while Art went to discuss matters with Linda.

"Thank you, Daddy…I love you," she whispered miserably as he left the room.

CHAPTER 23

EXPOSING THE LIE

"John, I had to come see you straight away," said Art to Pastor John Meade. John looked edgy even before Art started the conversation, which was unusual because he was known as a man who was always cool and in control; he was never caught off guard. Art proceeded to tell Pastor Meade all that Kate had told him. He did it delicately and respectfully, but he left no room for inaction – this was a problem to be addressed firmly and immediately.

Art could tell that John Meade wasn't buying it; he even seemed a bit remote and distracted considering the scale of the matter Art had just outlined. In spite of his pious reassurances, Art could tell that John was both sceptical and distracted as he spoke. He promised Art he would get to the bottom of it and would phone him tomorrow to discuss his intentions for dealing with it.

Strangely, none of it came as a surprise; Art felt that The Great Love had prepared him for John's response, and so he nodded his thanks and left the church office. Art felt a great peace in the face of all that was happening, as if The Great Love had it all in hand and all Art had to do was step back and allow him to handle it. So he didn't dwell on it much that evening or during the course of the next day; he simply waited – not so much for Pastor Meade as for The Great Love.

Art was beginning to understand something new; that circumstances cannot hold us if we allow The Great Love to hold us – and so he shifted his gaze from the circumstances and quietly waited for The Great Love.

The phone rang at eight o'clock on Monday night, and Pastor Meade, in brittle terms, reported to Art how he would be dealing with the matter: "I have discussed the issue with Dylan, and he assures me that Kate is making all this up to spite him because he refused her advances. I have also felt it necessary to discuss such vicious accusations with the church board, and we feel obligated to ask you and your family to take a step back from church life until Kate sees the error of her ways and repents."

Art felt a righteous indignation rise up in him. The response was both unjust and unkind.

But his heart reported something more important than the unfair actions of John Meade; it told him that he should give it over to one greater than himself. A few weeks earlier, this would have knocked Art for six, but in his heart he knew this was all part of a much bigger issue that must be allowed to play itself out. So he announced to the family that they were taking some time off church. He didn't ask Kate if she needed to reconsider and possibly repent; that thought never even crossed his mind – he just made his announcement and went back to reading his favourite book.

A short while later, Kate stood up to head off to bed.

"You okay, sweetheart?" Linda asked.

"I guess I'm okay, Mum, but I'm still fuming – it's not how I would have preferred things to turn out, but thank you for not doubting me anyway."

Art spoke up. "Kate, I said to you yesterday that this would end last night, and as far as I am concerned, it has ended. But I feel in my heart that there is something much bigger at play, and it's important for us to resist the temptation to get revenge or speak badly of Dylan or anyone else concerned – do you think you can do that, Honey?"

It took Kate a little while to process what her father was asking her, but eventually, against all her headstrong instincts, she slowly nodded her head and agreed with her Dad – and she lowered her guard and hugged both her parents to seal their agreement.

"That was a big thing to ask of a fifteen-year-old girl who has been so badly wronged," remarked Linda after Kate had left the room, "yet I feel like this will turn into a time of real growth for her. We just have to support each other until this storm blows itself out I guess."

"The Great Love has got this, Linda – we don't need to worry," assured Art.

But a mother's heart is not so easily calmed, and in spite of her confidence in The Great Love, she couldn't help but fret for her wronged daughter and the storm ahead.

When Kate went to school the next day, the storm raged. If it wasn't someone defending Dylan Meade, it was someone else calling Kate smutty names – it seemed that Dylan didn't take long to get the social media network active, and it hit Kate like a train. But she took it. She remembered her dad's words and let it all wash past her; she didn't bite back, and she didn't even give her side of the story. Somehow, in spite of herself, she just allowed it to run out of steam.

Linda picked up Kate from school instead of letting her walk home knowing that she would have to walk past the pastor's manse. "Are you okay, Kate? How did it go today?" Linda asked with all of the concern that had filled her that day.

"It was pretty tough for a while, but when I didn't bite back, it eventually settled down. By the end of the day, things were almost back to normal – but thanks for picking me up. I'm ready to be away from it all.

"I think Dad was right; there is something going on here that is not about me. I can just feel it – and besides, when I decided to not react to what people were saying, a strange peace came over me, kind of like I was an observer rather than a victim."

"I know that feeling, Kate" confided Linda. "I felt it quite recently when something that was buried in my past came to the surface. It was like I was looking at my life from outside myself – and I was held safe from the pain of it."

"Wow, Mum, that's exactly what it was like. I've never felt that way before; it really surprised me…in a good way," said Kate, allowing her guard to slip a little further. Linda smiled that smile, and Kate gave her one back. Linda suppressed the urge to flood Kate with all that had happened in their family over the past months – she knew The Great Love had it all in hand.

While Linda and Kate were enjoying the warmth that passed between them, Art was in another place altogether. The same tension that Kate endured at school seemed to have descended on Art's work place like a threatening black cloud, a cloud that would dump its load and soak anyone in its path at any minute…and Art just happened to be in its path. He went through his work day with the shadow of impending trouble lurking behind him, and at knock-off time, the cloud burst.

Art's return home wasn't quite so upbeat as Kate's. "It seems the Meade's have friends in high places" related Art. His boss was John Meade's brother-in-law and, after a bumbling speech about times being tough, Art was terminated from his job. "He couldn't look me in the eye the whole time he did it, and when I asked him if this was connected to a family matter, he began to shake all over – something very strange is going on, Linda, and it's much bigger than Kate or me."

Once again Art wrestled with the indignation of it all; it just wasn't right or fair, and once again the Voice assured him that his best course of action was to hand it over to one stronger than him.

As a family they discussed how they would manage financially around the dinner table, and all agreed to pitch in and get through it together. Art was sure he could pick up some casual yard work, and with a little tightening of the belt, they would manage.

"Can you feel it?" asked Kate. "The peace is here again. I just know this will all work out."

"Huh, I didn't know you could feel it too, Kate; that is so cool," grinned Stevie.

Tuesday morning started in a way Art and Linda were not prepared for. After the kids had left for school, Art and Linda had a second cup of coffee and discussed how best to find work for Art. They were talking through the pros and cons of advertising for yard work when the telephone rang. It was Marjory from the book shop, who was surprised when Art answered the phone. She was expecting him to be at work. "I was actually planning to have a chat with Linda, but now that I have you on the line, we might as well discuss some ideas I have," she told him.

"Ideas? What's this about, Marjory?" asked Art.

"Well, as you know, I run the bookshop and was helping Linda find the book on literature and poetry for you. As we were talking, Linda let slip that you had an interest in teaching."

"Okay, I'm following you so far; go on," urged Art.

"What you may not know is that I also run the adult night class education program over at the college and, for some unknown reason, we have been very heavily booked this year with enrolments in our Literature Appreciation course. Unfortunately, our instructor for this course called me yesterday afternoon to advise that his family who live out of town need him to move in with them for the next six months, so he won't be able to run the course – and immediately after he hung up, I thought of your name. Now I know you are not a trained teacher, but the course has already been fully prepared; we just need someone with a love for literature to sit in and run it – and if you like, you might even consider a short course in teaching yourself. Art, I'm in a real fix, and I know you could do it. The course starts next week; it's a paid position – what do you say?"

Art was completely caught off guard; this was not even on his screen, "Can I discuss this with Linda and call you back?"

"Sure, but I need your answer today, in case I need to keep looking. By the way," Marjory continued, "I heard the police arrested an old man at Pastor Meade's place last night. I hope everything is okay. Well, bye for now, Art. I'll be looking forward to your call later."

Art sat back down at the table and took Linda through all that Marjory had said. "You should do it" urged Linda. "I said that when you first talked about teaching, and I mean it; you would be great – and besides every little bit of income helps at the moment."

Art was torn between his lack of self-belief and a strange new excitement that he might actually be able to follow his heart after all this time. It all seemed so surreal; he hadn't even actively pursued this line of work. It was more like it pursued him and jumped into his lap as if it had a mind of its own. *Maybe that's how things work in the River of Life?* he wondered.

"Okay, that settles it, I'll do it. Oh, and Marjory mentioned something odd at the end of our call; she said an old man had been arrested by the police last night at Pastor Meade's house."

"That is odd" agreed Linda. "I guess we'll hear soon enough what it's all about; the rumour mill is very busy in this little town of Allanswood."

Art phoned Marjory back and accepted the offer, and he couldn't resist asking why she had thought of him for the job. She replied that she didn't really know – it was like it just jumped into her mind. With that settled, he decided to start on his own yard and spent the rest of the day mowing and weeding till the kids came home from school.

Pulling weeds is a mindless task. Art's thoughts drifted among the events of the past few days. His contemplations seemed to settle on the Meade family and roost there like a chicken that had settled in for the night – not that he was deliberately examining their lives, but more that he was tenderly brooding over them…to carry the chicken metaphor a bit further.

Something is not right in that family; they seem so competent and together on the outside, but it seems like a show put on by cardboard cut-outs, he mused. And as Art looked more closely at the cardboard cut-outs, a different impression came to mind – he saw angst clothed in civility, discontent clothed in piety, and most of all fear clothed in the pretence of conformity and order.

The Voice was showing him the truth that was hiding and simmering beneath the surface; and in that moment, he understood that religion had a way of forcing people into a mere semblance of all that it promises if they do not understand the truth about The Great Love. All Art knew was that things were not as they seemed in the Meade household and that trouble lay ahead. As he was considering these things, he heard the front gate slam as the kids arrived home from school and wandered inside to meet them.

Kate and Stevie were busting with news.

"Apparently Dylan Meade's grandfather was arrested by the police last night, but nobody is saying why," related Kate.

"Dylan Meade's grandfather? You mean Pastor Meade's father?" questioned Art.

"No, it's Mrs. Meade's father," replied Kate.

"I don't even know her father; and I've never heard of him being around here either," Linda put in.

"Well, that's who it was, and people are saying that the Meades were hiding him from the police in their house and that he was running from the law. It must be awful for them, in spite of all that's happened lately with Dylan," said Kate thoughtfully.

"Okay, kids, let's drop it now – it sounds like there is as much guesswork in this as there is fact. Let's just keep an open mind and hope this isn't as bad as it sounds."

But the following morning's newspaper headlines said it all: "Paedophile arrested while hiding out at Pastor's house." This looked very bad for John Meade and his family. This was the big thing that he knew in his heart was behind Kate's problem, their rejection by the church, and his subsequent dismissal at work – this was the real problem, and he was glad The Great Love had prepared him in advance.

Yet he knew that the storm now brewing around the Meade family was far greater than the storm that Kate had faced just a few days earlier, and he wondered how they would survive it; he also wondered if he could somehow be of help to those concerned. But he was on the outer now, and no such opportunity to be of help was likely, so he left it all with The Great Love.

The family talked about it over breakfast and decided together to do their best to minimise any gossip they heard and to encourage people to be considerate of the Meade family where possible. But Art knew how these things worked, and before long the police would ask very difficult questions of the Meade family, and his old boss too, and the church board would meet to ask for John Meade's resignation. But even more than that, there were the victims – whoever they were – and their own trauma, both past and present to be considered.

A heavy cloud seemed to hang over the town; everywhere Art went, he saw people in little groups talking with lined faces – some sad, some angry, and some spiteful. *Could The Great Love make something good out of this terrible situation, and could our town be the better for it?* he pondered – and the thought occurred to him that the River of Life contained healing for everyone, if they would just let go and receive it.

After putting a small advert for yard work up on the community noticeboard, Art had received several enquiries and was already into cutting his second house lot of grass for the day when he felt his phone vibrate in his pocket. It was the local newspaper who had picked up the story about Kate and Dylan Meade and wanted him to comment for a follow-up article in the next day's paper. Art saw red. He went through that reporter like a dose of salts. "How dare you rake up more mud when that family is already suffering under an unbearable load!" But the reporter cut him off mid-sentence.

"Haven't you heard, Mister Linden? Dylan Meade has just told the police that he was one of his grandfather's victims." Without missing a beat Art leapt upon the reporter's vicious search for more headlines and told him to never, ever call again.

"That poor boy," thought Art, "no wonder he is so messed up about sexuality." Art decided to finish up the yard and pack up his mower early to go home and get some peace with his wife.

"Cup of tea, Art?" she asked as he walked in the back door.

"It's just so sad, Linda" he began, then recounted his conversation with the reporter. "That poor boy, living there under the same roof with his grandfather while his own parents gave refuge to the very man who had violated his innocence. It must have been horrible for him. No wonder he acted the way he did to Kate; he is damaged and hurting beyond belief."

"Yet how wonderful that The Great Love knows," comforted Linda. "He saw my pain and healed me beyond my wildest expectation – and he can do the same for anyone else who lets him."

Kate and Stevie wandered into the house forlornly. Kate was particularly emotionally drained from the day's conversations.

"It was relentless, Mum" she related. "All of the people that lashed out at me and defended Dylan on Monday did the opposite today. They turned on Dylan with a spiteful vengeance – but I don't think it's fair, Mum; I don't think he could help it – and I'm confused and don't know what to do to help."

Kate ended by sobbing in Linda's arms until all the tears were spent, and then Linda began to tell her about The Great Love.

CHAPTER 24

LOST AND FOUND

They talked on and on about The Great Love, the River of Life, the Voice, and of course the talking fish. Linda told her everything…all the things that had happened to Stevie and herself and Art, she didn't miss out a single detail because she knew that Kate was a strong-willed girl who would need to be well informed to be able to submit her will into the care of The Great Love.

Eventually the boys had made so many comments about being hungry and wondering aloud what they were having for dinner that Linda sent them off to get fish and chips.

"Mum, this is unbelievable." Kate was deeply affected by what Linda had related. "I knew something unusual was going on in our family, but this is all so crazy and weird. Yet deep in my heart, I feel like it is true as well – I just don't know what to do about it."

"I've told you all this because I think The Great Love wants to fill you with his life; he wants to do that for no reason but that he loves you and he created you to live that way. And then when you are filled with his life, I think he wants to heal Dylan – and you can't help Dylan in the way that he really needs to be helped without The Great Love.

"Yet, even though you have a strong desire to help Dylan, you will need to set that aside while you learn to hear the Voice and trust The Great Love – and you can only do this for your reasons, not for Dylan's reasons… because first and foremost, The Great Love wants you to receive his love," explained Linda.

Kate wandered off to her room to think about all she had heard, but not long after, she walked back past Linda in the other direction. "I'm going down to the river to think," was all she said.

The river had that effect on each of them; not so much the physical river, but the River of Life drew each of them towards it and called to their hearts to come. Kate wandered the river banks trying to make sense of all that she had heard from her mother – but it didn't make sense. Kate was impulsive and head strong, but this was calling to something much deeper than her adolescent impulsiveness. She didn't instinctively know how to go about responding to something so deep and gentle – she was more likely to act on the spur of the moment than thoughtfully weigh up the issues and form a more considered response. It felt to Kate like she was being asked to act beyond her years and make a decision that would be in effect for her whole lifetime, when all she really wanted to do was live for the moment and enjoy being fifteen. But somehow Stevie had done it, and he was five years younger than she was, so she figured there must be a way to be true to herself yet also embrace The Great Love.

Kate wandered the river banks for a long time, occasionally saying hello to someone else who was out and about. She looked around her at one point and saw a lone figure on the other side of the river, sitting on some rocks surrounded by bushes and invisible to prying eyes on that side of the river, but visible at a distance to Kate. She finally recognised the figure as Dylan, probably seeking refuge from the gathering storm in his little hiding spot. She waved casually to him, and he lifted his hand in subdued acknowledgement.

Kate knew in her heart this was not the time to do more. By waving to him, she had sent Dylan a message that she wasn't mad at him, and that was enough for now; so she turned and headed for home. As she walked along though, the Voice spoke so deep within her heart that she barely perceived it, yet there was no denying a thought that had come out of nowhere: "You have to be lost to be found."

What does that mean? she thought. On one level, it was obvious; no-one goes searching for something that isn't missing. But on another level, not so obvious; some things are missing, and we just don't realise. Dylan has been lost for a long time. Last week he didn't admit it, but this week as circumstances conspired around him, he could not avoid the truth.

But what about me? Kate thought. *I don't feel lost, but maybe I am and just don't know it.* She shrugged it off before she had gone much further and continued on her way home. But the nearer she got to home, the more the thought persisted. *Maybe being lost is not being unable to find your way home; maybe being lost is being in a place where love can't find you?* An urgency to be at home suddenly overwhelmed her, and she ran the last hundred meters as fast as her legs would carry her.

Kate came puffing in the back door, red in the face from running, but full of joy to be back.

"Hi, Kate. What's the hurry?" asked her mum.

"I don't know, Mum. I just felt I needed to be with you… like your love was calling me home, and I had to hurry to be in it."

"My love is always doing that, Kate; you are always somewhere in my thoughts, yet lately even more so as The Great Love fills me with his love for you as well. I just can't help it – you have my heart," confessed Linda.

"So being lost is like being away from love, isn't it?"

"Well, I've never really thought of it that way, sweetheart, but I guess you are right. If we can't hear love calling our name, then we are the most lost people imaginable," agreed Linda.

"But what about people who have been hurt by the people who should have loved them, like Dylan?" questioned Kate.

"Well, I think they invent a kind of love that's not really true love at all – and they hide themselves in that fake love just to survive."

"Life is like that, Kate; to some extent, everyone has a damaged understanding of love imprinted on their heart – that's why The Great Love calls us to himself, so we can know and experience real love. We were created for the real thing, not the broken version handed to us by the ups and downs of life."

"Uh-huh," said Kate, "that makes sense – Thanks, Mum."

As her 'out there' teen daughter headed to her room, Linda thought to herself, *Each person must make their own journey, and what a unique journey Kate is on.* Linda mulled over the thoughts they had just shared; she had been lost, too – lost in a world of pain. But now she was found in an entirely new world of love.

Kate lay back on her bed and folded her hands behind her head – she half thought, half spoke the words, "I wish I was lost; then The Great Love could find me."

Deep down she heard the Voice again. "Do you really mean it, Kate? Are you really ready to be lost?"

"I don't know," she whispered. "I don't really understand very well what all of this means. And I've never really felt lost in my whole life; Mum and Dad and all of the other important things in my life have always been there for me."

"There are two kinds of lost, Kate, and because you are in a loving home, it's hard to imagine that there could be a better kind of love to be found in than the one you already know. You are fortunate that life has not yet caused you any great pain, but eventually it will – however, The Great Love will never cause you pain, and his love will hold you like no earthly love ever can."

"Can you show me?" asked Kate.

"Would you like to see the River of Life now?" asked the Voice, and Kate whispered, "Yes."

The mistiness began to gather around Kate's bed; it swirled gently and lapped at her hand. Kate moved her fingers in response, and it swirled even higher, sweeping fluidly over her bed and around her body – it was light as air, but it had a way of tenderly drawing her in.

"The River of Life will never exceed your free will, Kate; you must step off the bed and let it carry you away if you want to see more." Kate didn't need to be told more than that; she had heard about this from her mum. She carefully swung her legs off the bed and stepped in. But there was no longer a floor in her room, and so she found herself floating and enveloped by the velvety mist and carried along by it.

The mist wasn't watery; in fact, it had no physical substance at all, but it flowed like water and seemed to be seeking and wooing her. It was a river, but not like any river Kate had known before because it didn't flow out to the sea. Its destination was the hearts of human beings – it flowed in and through people. It existed to convey the goodness of The Great Love into the hearts of his beloved children – that was its sole purpose.

Kate met little Linda and knew immediately who she was. Not only was the resemblance there, but more than that, she could recognise her mother's heart. "Your heart is so beautiful" said Kate.

"Yes," agreed little Linda, "The Great Love made me beautiful when I was first conceived in his imagination. He gave me himself, and now he continually fills my life with his love because I am so precious to him."

"So what is it that flows through the River of Life?" asked Kate, "Well, that's easy," said little Linda. "It's just perfect love, of course; it's just The Great Love's heart flowing out from inside him – he doesn't have to try, it just happens because that's who he is."

"Are you saying that The Great Love just loves unceasingly, and that the River of Life flows from him and into people whether they know it or not?"

Little Linda scratched her head just like big Linda had done; it seemed like a very unusual question to ask – a bit like asking if the sun is warm, or if water is refreshing – it just is, and everyone knows it. After a little while, she said, "I get it. You don't know The Great Love very well, do you, Kate? You seem to have some misconceptions about what he is like, and I think I know why – because life on earth teaches you something that isn't true about real love. In the River of Life things work differently than on earth – we don't do love, or show love – we are love. We just are because The Great Love is, all we do is let go and let his love have us, and he does the rest."

"Does that make sense, Kate?" asked little Linda, but now it was Kate's turn to scratch her head.

"I think so, but it's so different to what I'm used to that I don't really know how to make sense of all of it."

"I've got an idea," offered little Linda. "You think of a bad thing that has happened to you recently, and I will tell you how The Great Love was loving you at the same time."

That sounded like a good plan to Kate, and she had a very bad experience fresh in her mind to tell little Linda. "Well, that's easy," said Kate, "I was really upset when Dylan was so hurtful to me and spoke such smutty things behind my back. It was like I was a garbage bin, and he was dumping his trash all over me."

Little Linda reached out and held Kate's hand while she talked; she understood the pain that came with life on earth. "Are you okay now?" asked little Linda, once again showing a kindness beyond her years. "That must have been so hard."

"I'm okay, because I know now that Dylan was acting out of his own brokenness. He was just trying to survive his own pain, and I happened to be in the way."

Little Linda began to explain to Kate about The Great Love.

"He doesn't like to see people hurting each other, and he doesn't like it when they are loaded down with trouble or sadness either. He created all people to feed on the life that flows from his heart, but people feed on the good and bad things that happen to them instead. They can't help it because they don't know any better; people don't know how to be nourished by The Great Love anymore.

"The Great Love doesn't turn on and off the river of his love according to the circumstances people are in; he loves us just the same no matter what is happening. If things are going badly, it doesn't mean that The Great Love has turned off the River of Life; and if things are going well, it doesn't mean that he has turned on the River of Life. It just flows all the time because that's who he is.

"Unfortunately, people are more inclined towards being in their circumstances than being in the River of Life; they just don't know any better," Linda said. "They just don't understand that the River of Life can carry them through anything.

"When you were going through your trouble with Dylan, The Great Love was there with you; you just didn't realise it. The River of Life was flowing around and through you, but you couldn't see it – if you had seen it, you would have known that everything would be alright. Letting the River of Life have us makes everything alright because the thing we need most is to know we are loved."

Kate was surprised to hear such a confident and clear presentation from such a small one, but it was obvious that she was simply speaking the words of Life that came from being in the River. She was simply imparting a knowledge that was greater than her, because it was in her.

Little Linda continued, "People just don't understand how much better it is to live in the River of Life, even you're still carrying some reservations, Kate – but they are slowly falling away as you grasp the nature of his love. It is all a question of what we can see; if our circumstances loom large before our eyes, then we will try to pull The Great Love into them and have him smooth them over for us. But if the extravagance of The Great Love's overflowing heart of love looms large before our eyes, then we will hide ourselves in him, and the River of Life will bring his goodness into all we face.

"If The Great Love simply attends to our troubles as they occur, then we will not hide ourselves in his love; but we were made for that love, and The Great Love will not do anything to impede us from having it. So when trouble comes, his love continues to do what it has always done – it calls us to let go and allow him to hold us."

Kate's head was swimming; this was much bigger than she thought…and much better as well.

"Soon you will be ready to let go and let The Great Love hold you," little Linda told her, "but for now, rest assured that his love for you is relentless. You can step in whenever you are ready."

With that, little Linda kissed Kate and skipped off into the mist, leaving Kate still wondering how such a little girl could know so much and say it so well…and what she should do next. But she didn't need to wonder because she opened her eyes and found herself back on her bed with just a few wisps of mist still receding over the edges.

Kate knew she had been found and that her true home was just around the corner waiting for her.

CHAPTER 25

NEW BEGINNINGS

Kate's new home in the River of Life may have been just around the corner, but it still took her a little while to get there. She knew that living in the River of Life was much better for her than living as a regular citizen of the natural realm, but there was a lot that she liked about her present-day life; she didn't know if she was ready to give it up. Her dilemma wasn't helped by recollections of certain Bible verses like 'My kingdom is not of this world' – did that verse apply to The Great Love as well, and was he suggesting that certain things that were important to her about the natural realm didn't count anymore?

She understood from talking to her mum and from her own instincts that she must die to one realm to be able to live in the other, but there were lots of things she didn't want to die to, because she felt like she had only just begun enjoying them. All the things that entertain the mind of a fifteen-year-old were swirling around in Kate's mind…things like boyfriends, school, boyfriends, family, boyfriends…you get the idea. She didn't want to stop having fun.

Linda poked her head around the door. "You okay, sweetheart?"

"I'm fine, Mum. I've seen the River of Life and talked with little Linda, and she explained so much to me; but I still have doubts about whether I'm ready to die to this world."

"Tell me about that, Kate. You may have similar thoughts to my own; maybe I can help you understand."

"I'm ready to relocate my life into the happiness and safety of The Great Love, but I'm not sure I'm ready to entrust my entire existence into his custody. I don't want my life to become boring and held back when I'm just getting started, Mum."

"Hmm, I see what you mean, Kate," agreed Linda. "It's a problem for everyone in their own way because we all wonder what will become of the person we are now if we die to this world. And we like who we are, at least some parts of who we are – and it's hard to imagine not being that person. My experience is that I didn't lose any of myself; in fact, I found that by dying to this world, my true self was enhanced – it was like the addition of a part of me that had been missing my whole life. I was meant to have the presence of The Great Love living in me, and I was incomplete until that happened."

Linda continued talking, "You remember when your father kept staring at me after I had decided to live in the River of Life? He said that I had become beautiful, but it was more than that – I had become my complete self, and the indwelling of The Great Love shone through."

"So you don't feel restricted at all by The Great Love?"

"Not one little bit. The Great Love doesn't restrain us; he loves who we are. He just fills us with his life, and it enriches who we already are – it's like his love illuminates our being so that it becomes magnified, and the result is that there is more of us, not less."

"Wow, so you don't think The Great Love has any problems with boyfriends and stuff like that?" Kate asked sheepishly.

"He made you that way, Kate; he is not about to put restraints on the very design that he built into you in the first place – but he will enhance it in ways that surprise you, and he will enable you to be the best version possible of your true self. And that's very important in relationships, especially when boyfriends are involved." Linda smiled in affirmation and conveyed a restful confidence in The Great Love…and Kate knew she was ready.

"Mum, I think I'm ready; in fact, I know I am – would you stay here with me? Can you hold my hand while I die to my old life?"

So mother and daughter held hands tenderly as Kate crossed over from death to life. It was a solemn yet joyful moment; Kate said in a clear voice, "Today I die, so that I will be born anew. Today my old life as someone who depends on the natural realm as my source of life ends, and all that it has to offer I give up as the great truth that holds my life in place. Today I enter into my new life as a new person who is sustained by the life that flows freely to me from The Great Love; that is now my new great truth. This decision is final. I no longer live as my old self; I am now joined with The Great Love."

Nothing seemed to happen for a while. Linda and Kate just sat there holding hands and waiting. Far in the distance they could hear singing, and gradually the singing came nearer. Both of them instinctively closed their eyes so that the natural realm did not compete for their attention – they wanted to see what was happening with their hearts.

In the distance, a rolling cloud of shimmering mist appeared on the horizon; it was rapidly expanding in every direction, filling the whole world with its brilliance and intensifying with radiance as it approached them. Then the cloud stopped moving, but the singing persisted and grew in volume; and as they stared into the cloud, they saw a great mass of people from all nations and tribes marching as one and singing for joy to herald the arrival of The Great Love.

The joyful throng burst out of the cloud and marched forward. The scale of the spectacle was awesomely magnificent beyond words, and the sound of the singing and the marching feet was almost deafening – and then suddenly it stopped. Not a person moved, not a sound was heard, and gradually the huge crowd parted to make way for The Great Love. The looks on the faces of the crowd were palpable; the love that they felt for The Great Love poured from the expressions on every silent face, their countenance a mix of great affection and breathtaking regard all rolled into one.

And as Kate and Linda looked in awe, they saw movement in the crowd as it parted to make way for The Great Love. His glory was like a brilliant light moving slowly through the crowd towards them, pausing to touch as he passed those who were within reach, and then he appeared. Kate and Linda were so overwhelmed at his appearance that they fell down before him and wept for joy, yet it was an elation mingled with sadness. They were joyful because the beauty of his love was beyond measuring and brighter than all the stars of the universe combined, but sadness because he had borne all the pains of human history so that we might share in his astonishing love again, just as he had planned in the very beginning. He came right up to Kate and embraced her, and in that instant, she changed into his likeness – she had been transformed into her radiant and beautiful true self.

Linda opened her eyes first, and she watched as Kate revelled in her new nature; she was the same Kate…but more so. The radiance of new life seemed to intensify and magnify her being, so that Linda marvelled in amazement at her transformation. *No wonder Art and Stevie stared at me that day,* she thought. It was a completely captivating thing to behold.

Eventually Kate reconnected with the natural environment. She tried to speak, but no words seemed to be enough, and she gave up after a few stammering sounds and simply grinned from ear to ear.

When Kate could finally speak, she murmured in wonder, "I don't know why I was so hesitant. If I had known that being in The Great Love was like this, I would never have delayed; I would have let go in a heartbeat. I feel like I have misunderstood the most important thing – that The Great Love must give love, not because we are worth it or because he has a purpose for us to accomplish so that we please him, but because it is who he is – and if he didn't do it, then he wouldn't be who he is."

Kate pondered these thoughts over the hours that followed; the nature of The Great Love, the River of Life that flowed from his heart, and the quiet Voice that spoke to people about these things began to take form in her mind – and she began to see things as they truly are.

I had formed an impression of things by all that has happened so far in my life, things done and things said – both good and bad. Some of these things were in the simple events that happen every day, but others were more directly put into me by the words that were said by people I trusted – words that I didn't question because of the way they were said. But I can see now that most of these things came out of brokenness, not wholeness, because the realm of nature is broken – it doesn't know the truth. There is only one truth that I really need to know and that is that The Great Love holds me in his heart, and that his life flows into me continually as I live in the River of Life.

These thoughts swam around and around in Kate's mind, slowly recalibrating her, slowly renewing her thoughts to align with the truth and showing her another way to be a human being.

All thoughts of being constrained or held back by The Great Love had disappeared; she knew in her heart that in the act of giving himself, The Great Love had set her free to live the biggest life possible – a life that would be shaped by the indwelling presence of The Great Love, perfectly blended with the unique ambitions of her own heart.

CHAPTER 26

DYLAN

Over the days that followed Kate's transformation, she thought a lot about Dylan and the prison of pain and broken trust in which he was trapped. At times she spoke out loud to the Voice about this. At other times, her conversation was more internal, like a yearning deep inside her that could not be contained in words but instead was more of an eternal cry for Dylan that sprung from the indwelling presence of The Great Love. She sensed a sharing in The Great Love's heart for Dylan, overflowing into Kate's heart because they were bound together – The Great Love and his daughter united as one by the eternal love in his heart. And all the love that welled up from The Great Love also welled up in Kate, as if she was being carried along by it as the human vessel that contained it and carried it.

She was clear about one thing: The Great Love was the only solution for Dylan, and she had nothing to offer him in and of herself. Dylan's pain could not be healed by human kindness alone; he was broken and needed to be mended in the very deepest part of his being, which was far beyond Kate's ability to accomplish. Dylan's brokenness was like a prison, and only The Great Love had the keys – yet she was equally convinced that where she lacked ability, The Great Love was competent and able if only Dylan would entrust himself into that eternal competence.

About a week after the arrest, Kate saw Dylan again on the river bank and waved once again. This time, Dylan didn't respond; the sadness and pain seemed to have descended upon him even more – like a heavy coat that he could barely wear. Kate felt in her heart that Dylan was close to complete despair and was slowly spiralling into a dark and impenetrable gloom.

"Tell me what to do," Kate whispered. "I can't just leave him like that."

Kate felt the Voice say to her, "Sit down on your side of the river opposite Dylan, just sit there and let your love reach across to him." So Kate sat, and Dylan sat, and they were both aware that the other was there, and that inaudible words were being spoken between them. Several hours passed, and Kate didn't move from her spot other than to stretch her legs and back. She just waited for The Great Love to reach across the space between them and touch Dylan with his love. She didn't know how The Great Love would accomplish Dylan's release; she just knew that her part was to sit and be there for him – the rest was out of her hands.

Dylan stood up and left, just like that. He didn't acknowledge Kate, nor did he cross the bridge to talk; he just got up and walked in the direction of his house on the south side of the river and disappeared around the corner.

Although Kate would have liked a more direct response from Dylan, she didn't let it concern her – if The Great Love felt that Dylan needed time, then that was fine with her. She trusted The Great Love implicitly and knew his love could be counted upon.

The next day after school, Kate sat again at the river bank. She looked for Dylan and waited for him to sit in his spot opposite, but he didn't show up…although somehow she sensed that he was unseen and nearby. This went on for the rest of the week. Kate would come home from school, say hi to her mum and then wander down to the river and wait for The Great Love to reach across to Dylan.

It was a full week before Dylan appeared again, though Kate knew in her heart that he was aware of her practice of sitting and waiting. Dylan sat in his spot with his head down, ignoring Kate, pretending he wasn't aware of her presence. Kate sat opposite and waited, not looking directly at Dylan but not ignoring him either. Her presence there was all that mattered. The Great Love would do the rest; it was what he did.

Eventually Dylan stood up and stared across the river. Then he allowed his pent-up agony and fury loose and yelled, "What do you want?" It was a tormented cry of deep heartache mixed with bitterness.

Kate didn't respond; she didn't want to step in front of The Great Love and whatever he was doing in Dylan, so she asked the Voice to speak for her. "Tell him that he is not alone" said the Voice, "and then walk away."

Kate stood up and yelled across the river, "You are not alone." For a few moments, she stared into Dylan's eyes as best she could from that distance, and then she turned around and walked home. She didn't look back; she didn't check Dylan's response. She simply rested in the knowledge that The Great Love would see Dylan through.

The next day Kate returned to her spot by the river, and Dylan was there waiting for her. She had barely sat down when Dylan stood up and yelled out, "I *am* alone."

Kate waited and the Voice spoke to her: "Say it again; tell him he is not alone, and then walk home."

Once more Kate stood up and looked across the river; she waited until their eyes met then yelled at the top of her voice, "You are *not* alone." Then she turned and walked home. She would have liked to say more; she would have liked to engage in some sort of conversation that expressed her care for Dylan – perhaps even run across the bridge and hug him – but she trusted The Great Love and kept walking.

This happened in more or less the same way for two more days – Dylan yelling out that he was alone, and Kate yelling back that he wasn't.

On the third day, which was Friday, Kate sat in her usual spot, but Dylan was nowhere to be seen. So she waited. Ten minutes later, she noticed Dylan walking towards her – on her side of the river. He stood some distance off, close enough to converse, but not close enough to be vulnerable – and Kate waited.

"You don't understand, Kate. It's easy for you to yell out words across the river – but you don't understand how alone I am."

"You are right, Dylan, I don't understand. I'm not trying to tell you I understand; I am trying to tell you that you are not alone."

"Maybe I'm not alone in that there are people hovering around me trying to make me feel better and worrying that I might do something stupid – but I am alone because the thing that connects me to people was broken a long time ago when I was just a little boy. I am on an island by myself, and no one can come onto my island because I own it. Everyone that should have protected me was too busy to even care that my grandfather was messing with me."

"So, Kate, I *am* alone; and you don't have the right to say otherwise because you didn't go through it."

Kate knew she had no words for Dylan that would touch his pain, so she looked into his eyes and began to weep. She looked directly at Dylan as she wept, looking through her tears and into his broken soul. She said nothing; she just cried and cried…and as she did, Dylan's resistance began to fail. He visibly fought back his own tears, until finally he had no more resistance, and his tears came.

They came in great agonising groans and sobs, and Kate went to him and held him. As she held him, the flood of grief grew to a shuddering, heaving crescendo so that his whole body was wracked in the torment of it all, emptying itself of the burden of the abuse and emotional torture that it had endured for so long. Then slowly it subsided, and they both sat down, exhausted.

Neither spoke; words were not needed in the midst of such brokenness.

Dylan's composure eventually returned. Peace seemed to descend on him, and he stood up slowly, smiled weakly and thanked Kate and walked home.

Saturday started slowly. There were things to do around the house and pent up conversations to have with the rest of the family. Each of them had discovered new levels of joy and peace as they ventured further into the River of Life; each of them had a story to tell. Breakfast time was like a flood of words that had been dammed up in them for the whole week, and a riot of laughter, sharing, hugging and tears exploded around the table – so many people to love, so many stories to tell, so much overflowing gratitude for The Great Love and their new lives in him.

Eventually, after the chores were done and the family began to turn their attention to their individual activities, Kate and Stevie packed up his fishing gear and wandered off together to the river. They chatted like new friends and felt drawn together in a way that hadn't happened since they were little. Kate wasn't embarrassed to be seen with Stevie, and Stevie wasn't bored being with Kate.

It's true, thought Kate. *The Great Love doesn't take away from us; he adds back the things that we've lost, that make us who were really are.*

Stevie began to get set up for his best day of the week, while Kate set off to see if there was any sign of Dylan around the bend.

Dylan was there, on her side of the river, not hiding from view but out in the open where he could be seen. He smiled as Kate approached and invited her to sit with him.

They began awkwardly, but once the ice was broken, Dylan asked the question that was on his mind. "Kate, I have to know something; what happened yesterday?

It was like everything that was bottled up inside me all these years was released in a flood; how did you do that?"

Kate thought carefully about the question, not wanting to appear overconfident or speak too soon. "I don't know exactly what happened to you, Dylan; all I know is that I was told to tell you that you are not alone."

"Told?" questioned Dylan, obviously puzzled. "By who?"

Kate laboured over whether Dylan was ready for the truth, and whether he would think she was crazy; but in the end, what did it matter? The Great Love would show himself in time, and it might as well be now. "By the other person who was there…the one who went through it all with you," she blurted out.

"There was no one else there, Kate. No one stepped in to save me, no one went through anything with me."

Dylan was getting steamed up and was about to storm off when Kate said, "He was there, Dylan, and he went through it all with you. He told me to tell you that you were wearing a blue shirt and green shorts; he told me to tell you that your grandfather told you not to tell anyone or he would cut you with his knife."

Dylan was stunned into immobility. The scene returned to his memory like a flood of fresh pain, and he saw again in his mind's eye that what Kate had said was true. "Kate…how do you know that?" he winced. "I never told anyone what happened, or even thought about what I was wearing that day."

"The Great Love told me, Dylan; he was there."

"If you're trying to tell me that God allowed this to happen, Kate, then forget it. I stopped believing in God a very long time ago. As Dad stood up there Sunday after Sunday in front of the church and preached about his God, I quietly have hated God for letting this happen to me."

"Dylan, I don't know any more about God than you do; and I agree anyone who would stand by and let this happen is not worth knowing. I'm not talking about God…I'm talking about The Great Love. And from what I know from personal experience, they are not even related. Maybe one day a long time ago, they might have been the same person, but not anymore – not since people tried to box The Great Love into religion."

Kate didn't really know where all that came from. She didn't plan to say it – it just spilled out of her mouth without any real thought…like the Voice said it, not her.

"Okay…I'm listening, Kate. Let's forget about God; tell me about this 'Great Love' of yours, and how he was there."

"I've only known The Great Love for a few weeks, Dylan; I only met him in the week after my Dad spoke to your Dad about the things you were saying to me and about me. But in that short time, I feel like I have stepped out of this world with all its troubles and pain, and into a new world that cleans us from all the pain and suffering in the world and holds us safely in love. I don't know everything, Dylan, but I do know that The Great Love doesn't operate the way we were told God does, that he doesn't watch from the sidelines and snap his fingers when the mood takes him. Instead, he enters into the pain with us, and when we are ready, and we give him permission, he takes the pain away and draws it out of us and into own his great heart, and then washes us clean with his love."

"That's all very nice, Kate…'and they lived happily ever after'; but it will be a long time before I trust anyone again – even this mysterious Great Love of yours."

As Dylan stood up to leave, Kate said one last thing: "You are not alone, Dylan."

CHAPTER 27

WORDS AND DREAMS

Kate's words had become stuck in Dylan's mind, and he couldn't escape them. He would engage himself in some activity or other, only to find himself repeating the words over and over again in his mind. *You are not alone; what does that even mean, and why is it even relevant?*

That night, Dylan had a dream. It wasn't his usual nightmare where he relived his violation, but a new dream – one that took him on a journey into a far away, unknown country.

He dreamed that he was himself, the same young man named Dylan, but in a different time in history. He was standing on the docks awaiting embarkation onto a square-rigged windjammer, about to set off for a new life in a distant land. He stowed his few belongings and went back up on deck to watch his home country disappear into the past.

He settled into the long journey and adjusted to the rough and tumble ways of the sea, knowing that many months lay ahead, and that he was just one passenger on a relatively small clipper that was nothing more than a small speck on a vast ocean. There was no land to be seen and no other ships; nothing else existed but the great ocean and the small ship.

By and by, Dylan came to know his fellow travellers by name; he learnt their stories, what they were leaving behind and what they were hoping for as they talked about all their interests and dislikes. Dylan met one old man in particular who took a genuine interest in him, but he never learned his name – Dylan just observed the old man's daily concern for his fellow seafarers. Dylan learnt how to stay clear of certain crew members who had a nasty disposition and embrace friendship with those like the old man who seemed more honourable, but he never got to meet the Captain. For all he knew there was no captain; all he heard were orders shouted from the bridge by the Chief Mate, but the Captain was never in sight. Perhaps the Captain told him what to yell, but there was no way of knowing because the bridge was concealed from the direct view of the passengers.

Several weeks passed and then several more, and the boredom of life at sea began to take hold of him; he was lulled into the dazed existence of limitless ocean and wind. The old man would wander by from time to time and ask after Dylan's welfare, and occasionally the Chief Mate would walk past Dylan and slap him on the back as a rough seafarer's greeting, but still he never saw the Captain.

The tedium was interrupted by a patch of rough weather that set the ship against the elements. What began as a squall soon become a violent battle between David and Goliath. The little ship groaned and heaved under the pressure; sails were torn and rigging was ripped from its fixings. The ship felt like it might break up – but still the Captain was nowhere to be seen.

As the days wore on, the sun was lost to them; the semi-darkness enveloped the ocean on all sides, and the ship began taking on water – more water than could be pumped out with the manually operated bilge pumps. All hands were called to the pumps, and Dylan did his part, working frantically to the point of exhaustion to keep the ship afloat. Passengers and crew alike drove themselves to preserve their only hope of survival. Even the old man took his turn labouring with his last drop of energy in a vain attempt to keep the pumps ahead of the crashing flood.

That night, the wind blew itself out, and the seas subsided; the morning broke as a clear sunny day. But the mood of the crew was subdued; the euphoria of survival was dampened by the death of the Captain. He had died of a heart attack, they said, from being at the helm and watching over the ship for three days straight without sleep as he fought to preserve the lives of his passengers.

The Chief Mate advised the passengers and crew that the Captain would be buried at sea that afternoon, and they were invited to pay their respects on the mid-ship deck. The Captain was wrapped in a shroud with his hat on his chest, and as Dylan came closer to pay his final respects, he realised that the dead man was the old gentleman who had asked after his welfare so often. The Captain was not who Dylan expected him to be.

As Dylan was looking on and quietly contemplating this, to his utter shock, the Captain's eyes snapped open. He looked directly at Dylan and said, "Things are rarely as they appear, Dylan." He held Dylan's gaze for several moments, and then he laid his head back down, closed his eyes, and they slid him down the plank into the vast ocean.

Dylan woke from the dream in a sweat of confusion. Seeing the old man slide into the sea was so confronting and final; he had only just been looking at Dylan, only just speaking to him – now he was gone, and it was too late to ask what he meant.

What was not as it appeared? Is it somehow connected to Kate's statement that I am not alone? The sea captain was with him throughout the journey, caring and concerned for Dylan's welfare, but Dylan hadn't recognised him because he expected him to appear differently. *Perhaps that's it,* he thought.

He liked the old gentleman and felt good when he was around, but he found it hard to make the leap that the old man was also capable of bringing him safely through the storm. He expected a captain to be strong and decisive, not tender and caring. Dylan's expectations of people rolled around in his head as he lay there wide awake. He thought about his mother and his expectation that she would care for him instead of protecting her own father. He thought of his own father, and how he was more likely to portray a stoic religious leader than a sensitive dad. And he thought about Kate and how she waited on the other side of the river…separate, yet together; caring, but not pushing in…and not holding a grudge for Dylan's poor treatment of her.

As he lay there, he began to realise that his expectations were largely the overflow of his pain, and that his life was stuck in a cycle of continually reaffirming something that wasn't actually what it seemed. It was as if his pain had determined what was true, and now everything had to pass through the filter of that truth for it to make sense.

And if it wouldn't pass through his pain, then he discarded it as a lie.

Dylan admitted to himself that his pain was the opiate that dulled and controlled his existence, yet that admission didn't change anything; if anything, it just highlighted his desperation and the helplessness of his situation. Deep down he had always known he was stuck, but now that he had brought it out into the open and admitted it to himself, he was no better off – all he knew was that an event which had imposed itself upon him without his permission had now also taken control of his life. Knowing about it didn't actually help, because even that knowledge had to pass through the filter – inevitably turning it into even more futility.

Dylan tried his best to get his mind to process things differently; he didn't want to be so stuck. But his mind seemed to have become stuck in a rut, and all his thoughts eventually followed the same well-formed tracks which eventually led him to the same desperate place. *If only there was a way to make new tracks in my mind*, thought Dylan. *If only I could make things appear different than they always do…if only.*

Sleep finally returned, but Dylan continued to wrestle with the impasse in his subconscious thoughts. It was a swirling continuum of people and events; the captain was there, and Kate, his parents and grandfather – all of them had something to say, all seemingly asserting their point of view and laying claim to the truth.

Then in the midst of all the din, Dylan heard another voice pushing through his sleep and into his subconscious mind, so distant yet so clear: "There is only one truth that matters, and it is superior to every other word that has ever competed for your identity. You are loved by The Great Love." As Dylan lay there, that singular truth eclipsed all the lies that had been written on his heart, all the lies that had been shaped by his pain and brokenness, that had lodged in his heart over the years, were overshadowed by love. Then a deep sleep fell over Dylan as peace overtook the pain, and he slept the sleep of the innocent, refreshed by the greatest truth ever known to humankind.

Dylan's mother was surprised that he hadn't appeared for breakfast. He was always up early, not wanting to spend any more time in his bed than necessary, because his emotional pain was always nearer the surface when he slept. She called him to breakfast from where she was standing at the kitchen sink, but he still didn't appear so she peered into his bedroom to check that everything was okay and found him snoring comfortably – and decided to let him sleep and hopefully gain some long-overdue rejuvenation. He was still there when she had a cup of tea later that morning, and she wavered about waking him before she drove down to the jail to visit with her father – but she thought the better of it and let him sleep on.

At lunch time, she returned home with hot food from the bakery for the family and was surprised that no one seemed to be around. Once again, she crept up to Dylan's door to check if he was up, and the now-familiar snore greeted her as she pushed open the door. This time she went over to Dylan and felt his forehead to check that he wasn't unwell, and as she did, he opened his eyes and smiled at his mother for the first time in a very long time.

"Hi, Mum, I'm starving, what's for breakfast" was all he had to say.

Katrina Meade had always loved Dylan, but long ago a wall had sprung up between them that she had been unable to breech. The unfolding of her father's destructive life had finally given her some understanding of what had caused that barrier, and her heart was broken. She hardly dared to hope, but it almost seemed today that the wall had begun to dissolve while Dylan had slept for so long…at any rate, she surely hoped so.

"You slept in, Dylan; it's lunch time, not breakfast time."

Dylan looked at the clock on his bedside table. "Huh, how weird is that?"

"Well, hurry and get dressed; I've got hot bread rolls from the bakery waiting for you in the kitchen."

John came in from the garden, and they sat down together and shared a meal. Things had been uncomfortable in the Meade household since Katrina's father had been arrested almost a month earlier. Each one of them carried their own unique pain, guilt and unresolved anger, while fears for how this might all play out in their lives also persisted. John's position as pastor hung in the balance; he had taken a month's paid leave of absence soon after the whole thing had blown up, and he hadn't preached or contributed to church life at all while the church board considered the best way forward for all concerned. In a little over a week, it would all come to a head; the future of the Meade family would be announced. During this strange interval of time, John had gardened, Katrina had visited her father, and Dylan had simply disappeared for hours on end.

But today, they were together for a change.

"You had a good sleep-in, Dylan," remarked John, to break the silence.

"Uh-huh," was all Dylan had to say – but there was no sting in it; it was just an adolescent reply. "These bread rolls are good, Mum; we should have them for breakfast more often," he suggested with a cheeky grin…and the sombre mood was broken.

They talked casually, but not with any real intent because they weren't that kind of family. Just being around the table together was enough of a breakthrough for one day, so no one pushed it any further – no one was ready to talk yet about the elephant in the room.

As they stood up to go their separate ways, Katrina murmured, "Thank you both for such a pleasant meal together. Lord knows, we needed it. I think that some-time soon we will need to talk about everything that has happened to our family. I don't think we are ready to do it yet, but sometime soon we will be ready; and then we should let the conversation happen…and see where it goes."

The men nodded their agreement, then each of them peeled off to mull over their own fermenting jumble of thoughts.

As was becoming his habit, Dylan wandered down to the river – for some reason, the environment always drew him and seemed to offer some kind of protection from the immediate world when he was in it. As he rounded the corner from his house, he paused and looked out over the expanse of water that lay beyond him, and a strange sensation came over him. He was looking at the river but seeing something at a much deeper level, as though there was another river flowing deeper within the river.

It caught Dylan by surprise, because it seemed to be bypassing his senses and revealing itself directly into his heart.

Dylan edged down to his preferred hiding spot, dropped to sit on the ground, and stared – the river was there alright, but there was another current moving through it, sometimes flowing with the river and sometimes against it. The current wasn't physical; it wasn't another body of water moving about. The only way he could think to describe it was another independent yet completely connected dynamic – the river within the river was Life. It wasn't even the sum total of all the living creatures swimming about and being alive – it was in there at a much deeper and more profound level than that – like there was something in the river holding the whole thing together and giving it meaning through its invisible pulsating presence.

The more he looked, the more Dylan realised that he was perceiving something beyond the sensory and beyond the bounds of normal reasoning; he was actually looking into another realm.

Perhaps this is what Kate was talking about, he thought to himself.

What Dylan was looking at wasn't spooky or scary; it didn't affect him that way. Rather, it was more like a deep insight – he just felt like he was catching a glimpse into how life actually worked. He felt like he had been given an opportunity to see into something far more real than the merely physical; he was looking at the divine life that held everything together, both visible and invisible, and gave everything its existence.

Now, that is a lot for a young man of seventeen to just stumble into, but the deep pain that Dylan had been experiencing seemed to have placed him nearer to that place between the seen and the unseen. It seemed to have opened him up in such a way that glimpsing into another realm came more easily than is generally the case. It was as if all the pain and anguish that Dylan had been going through, followed by the emotional release he experienced with Kate had carved off his many layers of protection, leaving him both vulnerable and also more spiritually perceptive.

You see, Dylan had come to the end of himself…he had nothing left in reserve, no inner resilience to carry him or protect him – and this place of emptiness positioned him to see into the realm beyond. At least, that's how it seemed anyway. All of the usual self-made scaffolding that supports and protects most people had been dismantled by Dylan's inner brokenness, and so there was nothing in the way to obstruct his view. As a result, he saw things as they really were instead of as his self-management of life had reconstructed them to appear. *Most people are full,* thought Dylan, *but it is only in our emptiness and lostness that we can see past all that clutters and presses into our lives and catch a view of where the true life really is.*

"Things are rarely as they appear, Dylan." The captain's words rang through his mind. Now he got it. Just because something appears to be a certain way doesn't make it so; there is always a deeper invisible thing happening, where the real truth is found. The river within the river was that deeper thing, and it set Dylan's heart racing with hope that perhaps he didn't have to remain stuck. It pulled at his thoughts and inflamed within him a quest to know more.

He understood now that the natural realm with all its man-made systems and programs can barely touch the real issues of life, that it had no real capacity to perceive things as they really are – and so its remedies were superficial at best. His only hope of finding his lost self had to come from a source beyond the natural realm… he needed to find out more about Kate's 'Great Love'.

CHAPTER 28

THE QUEST

Dylan didn't know how to go about his new quest; it was not a subject that anyone else he knew had spoken about…except Kate. His dad, who carried the responsibility of leading Allanswood's largest church, didn't even seem to know about this stuff. Yet Kate, who was just a teenager, was all over it – go figure! He hadn't seen Kate today; perhaps she knew that he needed his own space. She seemed to know a lot of things that were way beyond the reach of a normal fifteen-year-old.

By now the afternoon was wearing on, and so Dylan stood up and climbed the bank that led him to the path back home. As he came around the front corner of the house, he heard voices in the back yard, so he quietly edged around the side of the house to see who was there. To his surprise, he saw Kate's dad, Art, talking intently with his own father. It sounded like Art had come around to clear the air between them because of some strife that had happened – and Dylan had a fair idea of what it was.

"John, we need to talk. I want you to know that the tension between us as a result of my conversation with you about Dylan's treatment of Kate, our removal from church life, and also my subsequent sacking by your brother-in-law – as difficult as they were at the time – are now all in the past. Maybe sometime in the future we can talk these things through and find some degree of resolution, but for now I can see that you were all under great pressure. I just wanted to let you know that I am here if you need someone to talk to. It's too much to bear on your own, John, even for someone with broad shoulders like yours – so reach out when you are ready. I'm here for you." Then Art looked his dad in the eye, shook his hand and walked off around the other side of the house.

As soon as he was gone, Dylan sauntered into the backyard casually as if he was just arriving home. "Was that Kate Linden's dad I just saw leaving?"

"It was," said John. "He came to offer his friendship to us in the midst of all this turmoil."

Dylan knew he had to say more, but conversations with his father were not their strong suit, and so it came out in a stammering way. "Dad…Dad, I didn't tell you the truth about my treatment of Kate Linden. I'm really sorry, but I think I was attacking her because of my own pain, and I made up everything I said about her. I'm sorry if I've made this worse for you."

John Meade pondered Dylan's words for a few moments before replying.

"Dylan, on reflection, I kind of guessed that; I just didn't want to face it. I think I just preferred the lie to the truth, and so I turned it into the truth for me. And I was so troubled about your grandfather and the pressure he caused your mother and me by being here and dumping his story on us, that I didn't really want the truth. It was just another problem that I couldn't deal with – do you understand, Son?"

Dylan nodded, "I do understand, Dad, I really do."

"What a mess," lamented John. "What an absolute stuff-up this is, Dylan – I think maybe the church board should sack me. I'm not even sure if I'm up to the task anymore. And more than that, Son, once we found out what your grandfather did to you, I should have cared for you better too. I have let down everyone who is important to me."

"The strange thing is, Dad, that I think this is all going to work out for the best if we just come out from behind all the walls we have put up to protect ourselves. I think we are going to be okay in the end, Dad."

"What do you mean 'protective walls', Son?" asked John puzzled.

"What it means for me," explained Dylan, "is that my life has been hemmed in by the worst thing that ever happened to me; it's like I didn't have a choice, and I was trapped in there. But I'm beginning to see that there is something even bigger in my life than that, something even more self-defining, and it wants to contain me as well – if I am brave enough to let it have me."

"Are you talking about faith, Dylan?" asked John.

"I'm not sure yet, Dad; I'm only just beginning this, and all the answers still lie in the future for me. But I think my past trauma has settled around me and added layers to me that I don't really want any more; I just want to find out who I am underneath the layers and become that person again.

"Kate Linden said something to me yesterday about 'The Great Love' – but she wasn't describing the God we know. She seemed to be describing this 'Great Love' from her personal experience rather than through a religious framework. So, I don't know if it's got anything to do with faith – at least, the way we talk about faith; it seems to be more about simply entering into his love."

John looked decidedly puzzled and maybe even a little perplexed by what Dylan was saying. "One thing is for sure," he responded, "there is something going on in the Linden family that wasn't there a few months ago. It's like they know something…but I have no idea what it is."

"I don't think they want to keep it a secret, Dad. Kate had a lot to say about The Great Love – but she wasn't pushy, like she knew I had to be ready, and that I wasn't yet."

"It's a lot to think about, Dylan. I don't know what to make of it all. C'mon, let's go wash up for dinner."

The Meade family sat down to dinner, and after John had said grace, the family conversation opened up where they had left off at lunch time. Linda spoke up first: "Linda Linden left me such a nice card in the letterbox today; they really seem to care about us." John and Dylan glanced at each other. "What?" asked Katrina.

"Dylan and I were just saying earlier that something seems to have happened to the Lindens. The family have reached out to each one of us now, which is surprising considering the trouble we have put them through."

"I wonder what's going on" Katrina murmured reflectively. "They were always such a timid family, almost brow-beaten by life; now they seem so assured and composed. Whatever could have happened, I wonder?"

"Kate has talked to me about The Great Love," offered Dylan. "Maybe they have all had the same experience or something." Dylan opened his mouth to say more but his self-consciousness at conversing freely with his family took over, and all that came out was, "Uh."

"What were you going to say, Dylan?" his dad prompted. "Maybe it's time for this family to talk more freely about all that is happening to us, like your mother suggested at lunch time."

Dylan picked his words carefully, "I had a strange experience today, a really strange experience, and I think that maybe it is connected to whatever is going on in the Linden family."

"Go ahead, Son, tell us about it," John encouraged.

"Uh, okay – but you will need to listen and not judge me, because I still don't really understand what it means." John and Katrina nodded their consent, and Dylan told them everything he had seen down at the river and what he thought it all meant…and how things are rarely as they appear.

His parents listened carefully and respectfully, and at the end of it all John said, "The River of Life that flows from the throne of God – I thought it was just a figure of speech, like a spiritual metaphor or something; I never thought it actually existed. You would think that as a pastor I would know all about all that, but I'll be blowed if that isn't the strangest thing I have ever heard."

"I know, Dad, but it happened right before my eyes; I don't know if it was a vision or what it was – but I know I saw into another realm where the real truth about us is found. The real truth is that things are not what they seem and that we are not defined by all that life throws at us; we are defined as those who are loved by The Great Love – and I think I need to find out for myself what that means…so I can start all over again."

The family went silent; this had now gone beyond the boundaries of casual speculation and conversation. It seemed that the real thing was now vying for their attention, and it had the potential to undo all that had underpinned their lives to that point if they were not careful.

They were all thinking the same thing: *This has the potential to change everything.*

Finally John said, "Thank you for speaking so plainly, Dylan. I don't know if this is what your mother had in mind when she said it's time for this family to speak freely about what's been happening – but I have a feeling that this is connected to everything that has happened to us. So let's sleep on it and give it tonight to settle on us; we can discuss it some more when we wake up tomorrow."

"That's another thing, Dad. I have never slept so long in my whole life as I did last night. I feel like The Great Love is already at work in me, healing me on the inside – it's like my heart knows something already, and my head is just starting to catch up. It's like my heart has always known The Great Love, but my head obscures that from me as it interprets my life through all the circumstances I am in."

John's neatly arranged mind was unravelling by the minute – this had gone way beyond his orderly management of life. In fact, he was beginning to think that the entire foundation of his existence was being shaken, so he patted Dylan on the shoulder and left the room to think.

That night he and Katrina sat in bed and talked long into the night. "A month ago I wouldn't have entertained the thoughts I'm having today; I would have swept them aside as trifling and unverifiable illusions. But right now I feel like I've been missing something, and I can't get past the thought that there is more going on than I ever realised. It's like I had God neatly contained in the religious box I had made for him, and I've just looked inside it to find that he's not in there. And worse than that…I'm not sure he ever was."

"I know what you mean, John; I thought God could be found in all the programs and activities we had carefully arranged for him, but now I'm wondering if I ever really knew who he is. I've also thought that if he is The Great Love and not the God we thought he was, then we have been missing the most important part our whole lives… and so has the church that we have been leading these past twelve years."

Those last words had a very sobering effect on both of them; the burden of the church and their position within it weighed very heavily indeed.

"I thought my job was to be strong and decisive," John explained. "I thought I needed to control everything and have the church follow me because I portrayed a leader who knew where he was going. But I feel like all I've done is lead them into my own perceptions, instead of their own personal sense of security in God's love. I think the church knows God according to how I have expressed him, and that is not even remotely close to

The Great Love that the Lindens seem to be showing to our family…and I can't figure out which is right.

"Is there hope for us, Katrina? Can we still do what we have always done knowing that we have messed up so badly with all that's happened these past few months? I really don't know what the future holds."

"Let's pray about it together before we go to sleep," suggested Katrina, "except I wonder exactly who I am praying to now. If God really is The Great Love, then I'm not sure the old ways mean much anymore." But she began to pray anyway.

"Dear God…Great Love…whoever you are, help us to know the truth and show us who you really are. We just want to know you, so please speak to us." She almost added, "Amen" but thought better of it and finally just let their request hang there.

Neither John nor Katrina slept much that night. The thought that there might be something more going on than they had known about during their many years of Christian service left them both stunned…and really even more than stunned. They were frightened.

Maybe Dylan is right; maybe this will all work out for the best, John thought hopefully – but his heart wasn't in it.

By five in the morning, he had had enough and slid out of bed quietly.

"I'm awake, John," Katrina told him. "What about a cup of coffee in bed?"

As they sipped on their coffee and continued to turn over the thoughts and events of the previous day, Katrina suggested, "Why don't we invite Linda and Art over for dinner tonight? In fact, let's invite the whole Linden family over and ask them what's going on."

It turned out that Art was teaching night class that night, but they decided to get together for a late brunch while the kids were at school. They didn't spend much time on social niceties but got straight to the point. Linda and Art shared their story from start to finish. They covered everything from the beginning of it all with Stevie and the talking fish, Linda's childhood pain of seeing the death of her mother, Art's controlling father and his unfulfilled ambition to become a teacher, and finally Kate's trouble with Dylan and the ensuing fallout – all of which culminated in each of them, one at a time, losing their lives in this world to enter into life in The Great Love. They described the River of Life and the extravagance of knowing The Great Love, and how each of them had died to their old life to take possession of the new. And ultimately how they were now completely overwhelmed with the joy of knowing The Great Love and would never dream of going back.

By the end of it, John and Katrina sat there dumbfounded. They had never heard an account like this in all their days of ministry. In fact, it seemed like they were hearing the good news for the very first time. It seemed to parallel many of the statements that Christians made about God, yet it left the Christianity they had known so far a long way behind in terms of its reality. This sounded like the real thing – which left John and Katrina with a serious dilemma. If this was the real thing, then what was it that they had? Did they possess nothing more than religion dressed up in modern clothes to look like the truth? Surely not?

These were difficult questions indeed. John and Katrina had never contemplated that there was more to Christianity than they had known for their whole lives; they just went along with the system that had stood the test of time and perpetuated the view of those who claimed to know.

There were so many scriptures going around in John's mind; they seemed to be pulling at him to rebuild his perceptions of God from the ground up on the one hand, and reinforcing his old point of view on the other. In fact, the whole thing was looking more and more like a house of cards that might come tumbling down around him any minute if he wasn't careful.

"I don't know what to say," admitted John. "The implications of this are enormous for me; I would need to start over, and I don't think I could do that. Everything I have stood for would need to be reassessed. And it's worse than that even: my whole sense of identity as a leader and minister is in question – and I'm not sure I know what would be left of me. Without that identity, I would be nothing; my whole life and work would be meaningless."

John seemed on the verge of tears when Art cut in, "John, you need to look at this from the perspective of what you will gain, not what you will lose. The things you will lose are the superficial securities that come when we construct our sense of worth from our service, achievements and position; but the thing you will gain is the immeasurable depth that comes from being loved apart from our earthly accomplishments. You have the opportunity to live as you were first created to, completely carried and held by a love that is far greater than anything this world knows about or understands.

"Admitting you have been wrong is such a small thing compared with allowing a love so great to hold you. But as we said at the start, each person must choose just as each of our family members had to choose; no one can decide for us to cast our entire existence into the care of The Great Love. You are right, John. You would become 'nothing' – that is, nothing in the sense of your self-made worth – but everything as one who has been made worthy by the greatest love in the universe."

Linda sensed that John and Katrina needed some alone time, so she told Art they needed to get back for when the kids arrived home from school. As they parted, Art said to John as he shook his hand, "Dying seems so hard until we grasp the wonder of truly living." Then he and Linda headed out the door and left John looking dazed.

CHAPTER 29
DYING AND LIVING

To say that John was challenged by the events and conversations of the past few days would be a gross understatement. The past month had felt like he was climbing a mountain, but this was like the last haul up to the summit…without any climbing gear. It was one thing to have the Lindens speak so enthusiastically about The Great Love, but quite another for him to abandon everything that had underpinned his ministry to have it. On one level, he was deeply moved and touched by all they had said; but it scared him to death on another level, and his real fears began to surface. He had spent the last month hanging on – just holding it all together and keeping the pressure of it under the surface, like he usually did when it came to coping with life.

The pressure, combined with his usual coping mechanism, made it so difficult for John to reconcile The Great Love with the God he had known his whole life that he found himself retreating back into the safety of his long-held theology; he found himself disagreeing with Art and Linda all over again just to hold on to his sanity and convincing himself that his initial rebuttal of Art was right and justified.

John was just a man – he knew that better than anyone – but the ministry required him to be more than just a man. He had to be right. And in being right, he had built the walls around himself that Dylan spoke of. Walls the kept away those who would invade his life and strip him of his sense of worth, walls that would keep out anything that threatened his ministry…even the truth.

It was a hybrid kind of sanity that John had developed to convince himself that he was in control, but deep down he knew that he wasn't – he knew that an internal conflict of monstrous proportions was taking place beneath his cool exterior, and it could erupt on the surface at any time.

John and Katrina passed each other like ships in the night that day, hardly saying a word and definitely not discussing the Lindens. Not that Katrina didn't want to – she was ready to keep exploring this new and exciting revelation; but not John…he was busy building a new wall around himself to protect himself from it.

Eventually Katrina had had enough. "John, will you stop avoiding me and talk about this?" she begged him.

"No, I won't," exploded John in a fit of anger that she hadn't seen for a very long time. "If it wasn't for your father, none of this would have happened. You should never have talked me into giving him shelter; he's just an evil old man who should rot in jail."

Katrina couldn't believe what she was hearing. All of the pious platitudes John preached Sunday after Sunday had flown out the window; he was lashing out at those he was supposed to love most, and his true colours were beginning to be exposed from behind his carefully constructed shell. "I have worked my whole life for this, Katrina, and just when I'm starting to be recognised for my ministry, your father goes and destroys it all! I've never liked him…in fact, I hate him for it!" Then John almost ran for the door and slammed it behind him as he left.

John felt urgently compelled to get out of the house. He was suffocating in it all…he needed some fresh air, he needed to breathe. For the first five minutes, he ran just to put some distance between himself and all that had gone wrong. Then he slowed to a walk and wandered the streets of Allanswood aimlessly. Eventually, the tension went out of him, and he found himself wandering along the river bank, feeling foolish for his outburst but stubbornly resisting going back home. So instead, he found a quiet spot and sat down to think.

I've always tried to do what's right. I've always tried my hardest to build the church and to make it strong and healthy, I can't do more than that; I've given it everything. And it makes me so mad to have two nobodies like Art and Linda Linden spout their new ideas as if they know what's going on! It's just not fair on top of all that I've been through. And their friendly faces and forgiveness make me sick inside, as if I need to be forgiven for anything.

John didn't particularly like the direction his thoughts had taken, and he wasn't especially proud of himself for it; but he wasn't used to being at this end of the stick – examining his own life instead of telling others how to fix theirs.

The ministry seemed to have done that to John; it had turned him into an immovable rock who had lost the ability to scrutinize his own life. It was his job to be right, and he had honed it to perfection and then carefully dressed it up in religion.

How dare the Lindens call my life into question by suggesting that I need to die? How dare they suggest that I should admit to being wrong?

John Meade had stopped being wrong a long time ago when he made his commitment to build the church, and it was inconceivable that all his years of service were founded on nothing more than shifting sands – he simply wouldn't have it.

But in spite of his best efforts, John was tiring; he didn't know how much longer he could fight this thing. He didn't know if he could keep up his internal tirade of indignation much longer. His ability to contain the internal battle that raged beneath the surface was slipping…and he knew it.

Maybe I do need to die, he thought weakly. *Maybe I should just walk out into the middle of the river and get it over with – who would care, who would even notice how hard I've tried? It would serve them all right to find me floating in the water; then they wouldn't be so smug after all I've done for them.*

Suicide had never crossed his mind before. He was one of the strong ones; he didn't show weakness – at least, he hadn't until now. But what would his life be worth if he did? And would God consider his life of service to be sufficient to get him into heaven in spite of his miserable closing chapter? Would all the good he had done and the years of service be sufficient to outweigh his faltering at the last hurdle? John Meade decided he just didn't know.

God was always strict about things like that…messing up at the eleventh hour and letting him down in front of everyone. God wouldn't take that lightly, and why should he? He sent his Son so that we would get our act together and not fall apart – that's what Christianity was all about, toughing it out for God so that he would be happy with us…wasn't it?

So in spite of the fact that John was contemplating taking his life, he wasn't game to in case God was displeased… so he sat there more miserable than ever – hemmed in and trapped by the very beliefs that were supposed to set him free. And the battle that raged finally reached the surface for John to observe for what it was, and he didn't like what he saw: the very same religion on which he had staked his life had damned him.

"I just want to die," John moaned. "I just want to end it all and be free – but I can't because I don't want to go to hell."

"If only you would let me die. If only you would allow me this last favour, I would serve you in heaven for all eternity," he pleaded…but there was no reply.

Even as he said it, John felt foolish; he knew deep down that it was wrong to beg God. But the need to die persisted; he couldn't shrug it off in spite of the eternal dilemma it posed. He just couldn't escape the notion that he should die.

His thoughts returned again to the conversation with the Lindens and how each of them had died to this world that they might be born anew into the River of Life. He had to very deliberately keep his anger in check so that it didn't interfere all over again; but there was something they had said about dying, and he needed to think it through in the light of his own thoughts about mortality.

The paradox was that John wanted to take his own life and end his time on earth just to escape the pain of living – but he couldn't do that because of God's judgement. Yet The Great Love offered John a different kind of death that would enable him to live through it all as a new re-born man.

It seemed to come down to John's source of Life: was it self-made or did it come from beyond him. Did John really think he had the internal capability to do enough to get God to show up, or did he have to die to all that so that the River of Life might flow in and through his life?

"Am I prepared to die, that I might have life?" he muttered to himself dumbly. It was an important question for John because he realised that the term 'born again' was no more than a label to him; it was just a term that described the commitment he had made all those years ago when he was a boy, but there was no actual dying involved – just more determined living.

And who exactly is this 'Great Love' that I should consider dying in order to have him?

Round and around went the questions.

I know that I already believe in God, he thought, *but I feel like this is beyond believing in a theology – it is letting God hold me, instead of me holding God. It is to exist in a way that is no longer about me and my purpose, but him and his love.*

After John had gotten to the end of his ability to rationalise his way through and accepted that this was beyond his normal powers of reasoning, he simply admitted it – he just said out loud, "I have got no idea; if you want to love me, then you are going to have to show me what's really true."

It wasn't fancy or impressive like his usual more public dialogue with God, which was crafted more for the audience than God himself.

Very deep down inside himself, much deeper than his intellect, and deeper even than the place where his religious faith was embedded, he heard a voice. To say that he heard a voice would be to put too substantial a point on it – he perceived a voice would come closer. It was like a voice speaking to him from a distant room, and there were too many closed doors in between for him to actually hear it.

But some part of him heard something, and John sat absolutely still and listened. He didn't strain to listen; he just stopped his mind from doing what it did and let the voice find him if it could.

The Voice was determined to find John – perhaps even more determined than John was to hear it – and eventually the obstacles in John's mind gave way, and a faint but clear thought arrived on the doorstep of John's consciousness.

"Let go, John. Let go of all your competence. Let go of your reputation and your achievements; you have absolutely nothing worth holding on to, nothing to bring to the table. Come as a child with nothing in your hands – nothing in your hands, but trust in your heart.

And when you come to me empty of yourself, I will fill you with myself, and you will be complete. I created you to be nourished and energised by my love, not your self-effort or accomplishments. It is your true design; let it all go and come home to me, and I will give you joy and peace beyond your wildest dreams."

"But don't you want me to serve, and minister, and help the needy?" John stuttered.

"You are the needy one, John, you have defined yourself by what you give to me and to others; but your true design is that you are a vessel to be filled up with my love – and when it finally fills you to the top, it will overflow to others in spontaneous works of love, which is how I made you. At the moment, your identity is built upon your own life of good works in the realm of nature, but long before that defined you, my love held you deeply in my eternal heart. Your true self is more ancient than even the realm of nature; you have existed in my love from before time began, and it is only in my love that your true self can be found."

This was beyond theology, beyond the institution called religion that men had constructed to contain God; this was a love so refined that it existed outside of all the protocols of human life, yet reached into human life to express itself. This was Love, whose name was God, and who emanated Life…and this love was inviting John to come.

Still John's internal debate continued. "But this is too easy."

The Voice countered with the obvious: "If it is so easy, why are you finding it so hard?"

"The Great Love is ready to have you, John; all that stands in the way is your reluctance to have him on his terms – for free. He cannot remake his love with a price tag that you can pay; it is already the costliest treasure ever given to humanity – and the price is himself. You cannot add to that, John; all you can do is die to your self-made worth in order to have his free love.

"But enough of this circular conversation. You asked me to tell you what is next, and I will – it is time to die that you might live. You can do it now, or you can do it in twenty years. It is up to you when you do it – choose to be stubborn, or choose to let go – but eventually you must die or you will remain as you are: loved…but living as if not."

That was all John heard from the Voice. There was no more to be said, and John knew it. The next move was his. It was now up to him to entrust his existence into The Great Love or continue wrestling with life in the hope he might occasionally win a few rounds.

So he wandered back home, bewildered and ashamed of himself, and retreated to the back porch where he hoped Katrina might find him and help to unravel his confusion. Deep down, John knew he was the problem; but he was so unaccustomed to admitting failure that he didn't know where to start.

Katrina heard John shuffling about. She knew him well enough to know that she would have to help him because he was too proud to help himself – so she joined him on the porch couch, and they sat quietly for a little while, not knowing how to go forward.

What finally did it for John was when Katrina began to explain to him all that had happened since he had burst out of the house that morning. She explained that a Voice deep inside her had told her to rest because John needed to go through this on his own; he needed to get to the end of himself so that he could admit he had nothing to offer. There was nothing in himself of any worth in spite of his hard work, achievements and reputation – and that true life came from a source beyond his natural abilities…it came from The Great Love.

So they looked at each other like two little children embarking on an adventure together. They held hands and smiled timidly at each other; they emptied themselves of all their earthly securities, all the props that they had fashioned around themselves over a lifetime of Christian activities, and together they died to this world to become citizens of another realm.

To any observer who might have passed by, they were just two people holding hands while sitting on the cane couch on their back porch – but in the realm of the spirit, they were soaring through eternity. They had crossed over; the realm of nature could no longer hold them anymore than it could hold The Great Love himself – it was just a place that they would come to as the physical expression of their true existence in the River of Life.

They allowed the currents of the River of Life to carry them back to their origins, all the way back to their eternal home until they were face to face with The Great Love. And as they beheld him, they discovered that he was nothing like what they expected – because the brokenness of human reasoning had constructed an image of him that was not true.

Yes, there was a throne, but it was neither ostentatious nor the unapproachable throne of a judging King. It was inviting and overflowing with the lavishness of his great heart of love. And yes, there was glory, but it was not self-edifying or austere; it was a flood of goodness and mercy which knew no bounds. And yes again, there was omnipotent power; but it existed for the sole purpose of conveying his love into the furthest reaches of all his creation.

But most of all, there was a longing that his love would be received by those he had created for it, and that they would lose themselves in that love and have his life – just as he planned in the beginning.

So overwhelming was The Great Love and the longing in his heart for them, that John and Katrina fell down at his feet and wept for joy as it consumed and burnt up all the fears and doubts that had built up in them over a lifetime of broken thinking. He filled them to overflow-ing with his perfect love so that they shone with all the brilliance and perfection of newly fallen snow, and then together Katrina and John's hearts welled up and joined The Great Love in song as the longing of his heart met with their own and overflowed from within them. The ancient song of praise that had been buried inside them under the layers of their brokenness finally found expression again, and they worshipped him with their whole being because it could no longer be held back – such was the nature of their true eternal design.

To any observer who might have passed by, they were just two people holding hands and weeping quietly; but to those in the realm of the spirit who looked on in awe, they were the King's lost children who had come home and been crowned once again in glory.

They sat and revelled in the wonder of such love until eventually they were interrupted by the sound of Dylan returning home. He called out for them and found them out back holding hands.

"Come and sit between us, Dylan; we have so much to tell you." So they opened up a space for him between them on the couch, and as he sat down, the glory overwhelmed him too and he let himself be drawn into it; and together, the three of them cried at the feet of The Great Love as he poured his healing love into their hearts for all they had been through.

But for Dylan, The Great Love did something that he reserved for only the rarest of occasions. He took Dylan into his arms, and they wept together. The broken boy and The Great love wept until all of the brokenness had been exchanged, and so the broken boy was made whole by the divine life that was released from The Great Love as he entered again into the boy's pain.

And when they looked again at The Great Love, they saw upon him the scars of human suffering and understood the depth of his love that he would humble himself and allow himself to be crushed to bear the pain of his children. The nature of his love was clear now. It was more than benevolence or charity. It was the unstoppable urge of a love that could not be held back by mere human weakness, and it could not rest until the broken sons and daughters of Adam were back home in his love once again.

CHAPTER 30

PEACE LIKE A RIVER

Katrina, John and Dylan were so elated that they drove straight around to the Linden's to tell them everything. It was mayhem in the Linden's lounge room as each person talked over the other, each expressing the wonder of knowing The Great Love and sharing in his life. One moment there were hugs, then detailed explanations of what they had each experienced, and of course an abundance of laughter and tears.

When the initial excitement had settled down, Art and John moved into the lounge room for coffee while Linda and Katrina sat at the kitchen table enjoying a cup of tea. The kids had wandered outside to find their own private space to talk, so each person was now able to explore the flow of their own thoughts about how they felt and what it meant for the future.

Art began, "It's only a few days now before the church meets to vote on your future as pastor. How do you feel about that, John? Are you concerned?"

"I was concerned yesterday, but not today," John admitted. "I just know that my life is held by a love so great that my future is safe – whether that future is in the church or not seems much less important after today. I died to my earthly securities today, Art; the last thing

I want to do now is breathe new life back into those securities by grabbing the reins back – The Great Love has got me now, and I am happy to let him take the lead."

Art considered John's words and replied, "Even in the short time since I began this journey, I have already learned from experience that resting in the assurance that The Great Love holds us in his goodness and mercy is the best way to walk this out. Who knows? He may have something up his sleeve that you haven't even thought about. Take my work situation, for instance; I haven't missed a day's work since being laid off, and I have the added bonus of the part-time teaching work that I had always dreamed about doing."

John winced when Art mentioned being laid off. "Forget it, John; I have. We've never been happier."

"Katrina and I noticed that, Art; it's as if you have become the brand-new people that The Great Love first had in mind when he conceived you in his mind in eternity – like, his love is overflowing out of you without any effort. Your family have become so real and alive. If you don't mind me saying, you seemed a little timid before; now you exude such an easy confidence."

"You've got that right, John. I was scared of my own shadow a month ago, and now I feel like nothing can get to me. I just can't shake off the notion that I am somehow floating just a little bit above all the things that held me down and troubled me so much before."

The ladies came into the lounge room to join them, both full of their newfound friendship and the elation of knowing The Great Love. John spoke.

"Art and I were just discussing how this has changed your family, Linda, and how you are enjoying a whole new kind of happiness together; but it makes me so regretful for all the hardship we put you through."

"John, I'm not saying it was easy, but it happened at a time when I was just beginning to rest in The Great Love, and Art was on the cusp of his own revelation. So we found that it was because of our personal emptiness and brokenness that the layers that held us back were able to be removed – in that regard, our troubles at that time worked in our favour. We just felt so stripped of our own ability to manage life ourselves, that letting go made more sense in the end."

They each shared and talked about the letting go and dying that had been necessary for each of them, each in their own way, and with their own individual internal struggles to deal with – and they agreed that that was the common thread between them all: each of them had to die to be born back into life.

They hugged as they parted and promised to keep sharing as the days unfolded, but it was Dylan who surprised them all by saying, "I was so dead on the inside, and it was only your kindness that gave me another chance, Kate. I just wish you weren't so young!"

Kate blushed, and Dylan smiled awkwardly. What a day.

The week continued to unfold with new joys of discovery for each of them, but John's transformation in particular seemed the most poignant. He had an ingrained perspective of God that had been his beacon for his whole life, but over a matter of just a few days, it seemed to disintegrate around his feet – till all that was left was The

Great Love and the River of Life. And it showed; John was relaxed, and there was no fear about the future. Instead, he felt only a deep confidence that The Great Love held him safe.

As the week was drawing to a close, John had a phone call from the chairman of the church board confirming that a decision about John and Katrina's future at the church would be made at the special meeting on Monday night. John expressed his confidence in the church board and gave his assurance that as a family they were doing fine. Then a thought popped into John's mind, or perhaps a Voice, and he said without thinking, "I would like an opportunity to address the church for a few minutes at the end of the service on Sunday, if that's okay. Rest assured I will be respectful and brief." The chairman was uncertain if it was a good idea, but eventually relented because of the good standing John held with the church members.

"And just one more thing," said John, "I would like to invite the Linden family to attend church too as it was because of my family's troubles that they were asked to step out of church life – and I would like them to be there for what I have to say."

"Okay, John, see you Sunday," and he hung up.

John conveyed his request to Art Linden who was both surprised but also enthused by John's intention to speak to the church. "Wild horses couldn't keep us away, John." And it was arranged.

To say that the mood in church was sombre was an understatement; few people looked John and Katrina in the eye, and some seemed to go out of their way to avoid contact altogether. "This doesn't bode well for Monday night," quipped John to Katrina with a sly wink. To most of the church family, it seemed like the service went on forever; but John's heart was full of hope and anticipation, eager to share his few words at the close of the service.

The chairman introduced John and sat down as John was walking up to the front. He didn't go to the microphone but simply stood in the aisle near the front row and spoke.

"Thank you, friends, for the opportunity to say just a few words before you meet tomorrow night. I am standing here before you today to resign my position as your pastor. I have let you down, and you should not be burdened with such a heavy decision. In the four weeks since we have been on leave of absence, I have had time to reflect on many things – and the circumstances around my father-in-law's arrest, although I am deeply sorry for misleading you, is not what I am talking about. I have failed you as your pastor because I led you to believe that your faith is primarily about Christian service rather than personally discovering the wonder of living in your Heavenly Father's love. This may not make much sense to you right now, but it makes sense to me and Katrina, and we tender our resignation for that reason alone.

"As for tomorrow night, there is no decision to make about whether I should be dismissed because I have already resigned. However, I am willing to discuss with you in more detail my reasons for resigning if you wish – and if after hearing my thoughts we mutually agree to go forward together, then you may choose to call me to be your pastor. And if not, then I give you my sincerest apology and fondest wishes, and we will vacate the manse and leave. Good day friends, and thank you for hearing me out."

No one moved. This was completely unexpected.

The chairman stood up again, looking decidedly confused; he awkwardly thanked John for relieving the congregation of the decision and cancelled the Monday night meeting, "The church board will get back to you about the next step in appointing a pastor," he promised before he dismissed the gathering.

Art and Linda went to where John was standing and hugged him, and slowly others followed suit. Before long a crowd had gathered around John shaking his hand and asking questions about what he meant. "Drop in some time, and we can talk more," was all he had to say.

And drop in they did. Over the hours and days that followed, a constant stream of people called on the Meade family and listened with great interest to the story they had to tell. It became clear that the Linden family had experienced the same thing, and they also received more visitors to their home in a few days than they had entertained during the entire time they had lived there.

Over the following months, a new sense of peace descended over the church community and the town of Allanswood at large, and a wonderful transformation began to take place.

One by one, the church family began to die to this world so that they could be reborn into The Great Love. Before long, it was like a snowball that gathered up everyone that stood in its way. No longer was it dependent upon the Lindens or the Meades for its momentum; each person spontaneously shared the wonder of living in the River of Life. They couldn't help themselves, such was the joy that filled them; and so it spread through the church and then the whole community.

John and Katrina were unanimously reappointed as pastors to walk with the church family in their new life. The Lindens re-joined the church family too, and the life that flowed from The Great Love took over the township of Allanswood and gave it a new identity that was not tied up in its past achievements and disappointments. The town of Allanswood became known as a deeply contented place populated by people who seemed to know something…that they were loved quite apart from the best and the worst of their lives. They were loved because The Great Love gives love…it's just what he does.

Apparently, it's been happening in other towns and communities too, just like it happened in Allanswood. It just seems to start as people find themselves empty and lost and unable to fix their brokenness, and so the River of Life beckons and draws them in and fills them with a joy beyond words…and peace like a river.

Who knows where it might happen next? All I know is that it happened in a tired township called Allanswood that had had its day – and it began with a little boy who loved the river.

www.ingramcontent.com/pod-product-compliance
Lightning Source LLC
Chambersburg PA
CBHW070016120726
47909CB00003B/961